BGM & PLEX PRESENTS

GET IT HOW YOU LIVE VOL 3
The Gift and The Curse

Can't Stop! Won't Stop!

I0664863

By PLEX

BADLAND PUBLISHING, LLC

GET IT HOW YOU LIVE: The Gift and the Curse
Copyright 2015 by: PLEX
Written by: PLEX
Cover design by: Cedric 'Ckillz' Killings & PLEX
Graphics by: Cedric 'Ckillz' Killings
Book design by: Pam Quigley
Published by: BadLand Publishing, LLC
                       P.O. Box 11623
                       Riviera Beach, FL 33419
                       www.badlandpub.com

GET IT HOW YOU LIVE: The Gift and the Curse
ISBN: 978-0-9839123-6-1
First Edition

DEDICATIONS

I dedicate this book to Bernard 'Big Gemo' Moore. I love you, Junior!

ACKNOWLEDGEMENTS

God. I have to thank Him. PLEX. I most definitely have to thank me, because truthfully, I worked goddamn hard to become god with the pen. I'm ten novels in, five years in the book game, and finally you all are starting to recognize my work. It's a little late, but I thank you nonetheless.

Shout out to Darlene Gabo. You are a special chick! Thanks for all of the love and support that you give Junior. One love, lady.

One time for my man Ant at the G-Box (Booth F-31) in USA Flea Market. If y'all live in or around Miami, y'all go by the G-Box and shop with the homie! He's got all of the new CD's, DVD's, and BadLand/BGM/PLEX Presents books! So holla at the homie!!!

Chosen Books & Gift Boutique in MD... Black Stone Bookstore in MI... Dear Book in FL... Thanks a million for carrying and pushing SOMETHING 2 DIE 4!!!

To my two sets of extra eyes: Benny Redd and Mike 'Ball' Harper. I could not get these books out without y'all!

Nokesha Lee, Reginald Walton, Shaquana Killings, Cedric 'CKillz' Killings, Ms. Toni Doe, Elsa J. Joseph, Troy 'Des' Cannon, KP, Tron, Sleep, Lil B, Fat Rat, Trub Brown, Jit, Man-Man, Nephew Mal, Bino, K-1, D-Boi, CJ (Pimpin Ass Nigga Out of Memphis), Mike Brown, JG, Boosie Pless, Cool Ass Vert (One Blood!), Stacey, Jimbo, Pookey, Joe Hollywood, Dip, Ebb Rock, C. Ross, and Marcus Ray: Thanks for the love and support! In one way or other I owe it all to y'all.

Lisa Banks, Pam Quigley, and Tikeisha Reid, I love y'all for reasons that you'll probably never know. But I thank y'all with all of my heart. For not just being real with me [ALWAYS], but for just being you.

Chris Hayes. What it do, homie?! You're a real cool dude. I know I go hard on you at times, but it's all in love. Stay you, bruh! Do that and you'll always be loved and respected... One love!

Dawn E. Westbrook. Damn, baby, what's good?! I just wanted you and the whole world to know that I've ALWAYS been in love with you!!! Stay cool, sis.

Troy 'Disco' Jones. What it do, bruh?! I promise to God they're loving YOUNG-N-THUGGIN!!! You better get part 2 together... Love you, bruh!

Wayne E. Gladden, Cuda Hound, Chino, y'all are like the best friends God could give a dude like me! Thanks for everything! In due time I'll pay it forward, because we never go back. You feel me?! Love!

Capo Cat [Freeman]. I'm proud of you, bruh! Keep that pressure on the game! You heard me?! TURN UP on them... and One love!

Thanks to everybody reading this and everybody who has ever supported me or one of my authors... We really love and appreciate y'all...

PLEX [The Ruler]

OFF THE RULER'S DESK

I'm *Getting It How I Live* over here, *homes*! Money, magazines, marketing, and we're about to do the movie. Sucka free and striving for excellence! Just made payroll, now I'm vibing. Ended up asking God to alleviate my enemies and I lost two of my friends, but fuck 'em! Because it's only so much room at the top, you heard me?!

I started out five years ago with the end in mind, having evaluated and learned from others' experiences as well as my own. Got proactive — smoothed out the bumps in my path. Created a synergy — BadLand and Book Gang Media, two companies with one goal! I mean, really, that whole marketing plan was me, *homes*! And the fact that I'm winning, the fact that these hits keep coming out, shows that WE ARE successful over here on BadLand/BMG, Inc. Just think for a minute! Think about all of the books that dropped in and around 2009, then think when's the last time you heard anything from them...? Point seen, their loss!

We have something special over here, *homes*! We're motivated by a higher purpose — *sacrifice* — that willingness to subordinate what you think you want now for what you know you'll need later... *You see us now?!*

What lies behind us and what lies before us are tiny matters [when] *compared to what lies within us.* You heard me?! Oliver Holmes said it, but I live it! *Excellence.* Patient enough to wait for it, but too ambitious to become stagnant. Balanced, *homes*... You have to be balanced to truly *Get It How You Live*, because we are what we repeatedly do. Excellence, then, is not an act, but a habit. So y'all tighten up, get your minds right and keep it off of mine...

One Love,
PLEX [The Ruler]

Prologue

The big six-foot-four, 250 pound Hungarian stood before his followers. They were all congregated at a large, round table. The air was charged with nervous anticipation.

With his cold blue eyes moving from face to face, Kadar measured every man and woman that sat before him. Beside Kadar, the new leader of the Hungarian Mafia, stood his *consulere*, Ferenc. Ferenc was a small, nervous man. His eyes were dark and large. At 47, Ferenc had seen a lot in his years as a member of the Hungarian Mafia. Leadership had come and gone, yet Ferenc was still here. The small, nervous man with the full-head of gray hair was a survivor.

Standing opposite Ferenc, on Kadar's other side, stood Koka, Kadar's sister and second in command. Koka stood an even six-foot tall and weighed a sexy 133 pounds. Since junior high Koka had trained in martial arts and conditioned her body strenuously. So she wasn't just sexy, she was deadly. Her eyes were a cold blue just like her brother's. With measurements of 32-24-36, pale white skin and small lips, Koka was every man's desire.

As a rule, every man or woman in attendance wore black suits and ties. The Hungarian Mafia was one of the world's oldest mobs and their discipline was strict.

"Do you all know why I have called you here today?" Kadar asked. His Hungarian accent heavily pronounced.

Everyone nodded their heads. They all knew that Andras Simonyi, their previous leader and Kadar's mentor, had been murdered along with his beautiful wife April Simonyi. And though Andras' murder had placed Kadar at the head of their organization, it was easy to see that he was saddened by the event and wanted blood as a result.

"I know who is responsible for this." He nodded his head. An evil frown covered his pale face. Kadar was only 29 years old, but looked as if he were 40. The corners of his *buzz-cut* were gray and he had crows feet on the corner of his cold eyes. "I want them dead."

Again, everybody nodded their agreement.

"Now, none of you know this, but when our beloved Andras was murdered, three million dollars in rare diamonds were stolen," Kadar informed the captains of his mob.

A loud murmur buzzed throughout the room as the wide-eyed members discussed the newfound revelation. The Hungarian mob dealt in all sorts of vice: Extortion, human trafficking, prostitution, and murder for hire. But *blood diamonds* were their main source of income. And three million dollars' worth was a substantial amount.

After allowing them a few minutes to vent, Kadar began speaking again. "I've heard from my sources that a large amount of drugs were somehow surrounding this whole mess. I also have the surveillance tapes from Andras' house cameras. The people are Americans. Niggers! And I want them dead!" Kadar said, adding a string of obscenities in his native Hungarian language. "And I want those diamonds back!"

Kadar was furious. He removed his black suit coat and tugged at his black tie. The thin silk shirt stretched and strained to contain Kadar's twenty-inch biceps and huge pectoral muscles. A big gray-steel .50 caliber Desert Eagle was holstered beneath his left armpit.

A senior member of the board cleared his throat. The old Hungarian was bald and chubby. Liver spots marked his round face. "Kadar, it's forbidden for *any* member of this board to deal in drugs, and that especially goes for the *don*. Rules were put in place to safeguard this organization and to distinguish us from common nigger and spic gangs! So if Andras broke those rules and laid with *nigger-dogs*, who are we to involve ourselves because he got bit? I don't think this —"

Kadar pulled the big gun from its holster, causing the man to fall silent. His eyes bulged as Kadar briskly approached him. The room was dead quiet...

BOOK 1NE

...throughout history GANGSTAS have evolved in many ways. Like chameleons, they adapt to their changing environments... however, their current model seems to have unfolded its greatest extreme... GANGSTAS rose to their greatest dominance with the election of Ronald Reagan in 1980... now, anything other than maximization of profits is viewed as weakness. Any attempts at sharing what was 'taken' is viewed as an attack... GANGSTAS *get it how they live* and deal with all the attacks on their progress with swift violence and maximum efficiency...

—PLEX [The Ruler]

IT'S ALL ON YOU

Chapter 1

BG had dotted all of the I's and crossed all of the T's as far as business was concerned. He'd done his *Easy Rawlins* thing on the streets. The puzzle's pieces were all in place, he merely had to put them together.

Haitian Jack's complete estate was now in his possession. He, Monique and Devon spent every weekend there beside the pool, but weekdays were spent at her house because of Devon's schooling.

BG had everything that a man could ask for, yet none of it seemed to ease his pain. Today was JackBoy's birthday and it made things even harder for BG. Harder to function and deal with the pain of his substantial losses in life. *Damn, BG!* he thought to himself as he cruised down 79th Street in a rental. *How did shit get like this?* he wondered as Lil Wayne sang the hook to Game's hit single... *I'm grindin' till I'm tired/ but they say you ain't grinded till you die/ so I'm grindin' with my eyes wide... lookin' to find/ a way through the day/ a light through the night/ Dear Lord, you done took so many of my people/ I'm wondering why you haven't taken my life...What the hell am I doin' right?!*

His phone rang. The ID read PRIVATE...

BG answered, knowing that it was Haitian Jack.

"What's good, kid?"

"Not much. The lawyer you sent seems to be good. We discussed a lot."

"He's the best, kid-kid. I was about to give him some money for you, but he told me somebody had already sent him a check for $70,000. Look like you got some winners on yo' team kid," BG spieled, letting Haitian Jack know that he'd given Marquis Wimberly $70,000 for his coming murder trial. The feds had yet to touch the case, but everyone, Mr. Wimberly included, felt that they were coming.

"Yeah, and I really 'preciate them. How's the house, you like it?"

"It's aiight. A lil' small for a boss, but it'll do. You feel me?" BG capped and they both bussed out laughing. "Nah, man, I love it, bruh. I'ma hate to give it up when you beat them crackas and return to the streets. You feel me?"

Haitian Jack chuckled. BG was his man. He always talked so positive concerning Jack's case. That was something that he needed, because he had truly given up on freedom. And besides BG and the stripper chick, Nikkia, he'd severed all ties to the streets. He lived his life in between the steel bars of his cell.

"I hear you, kid," Haitian Jack finally managed to respond.

"Nah, nigga! Fuck that *hear me* shit. Do you *feel me*?" BG shot back.

Haitian Jack laughed. "Yeah, kid-kid, I *feel* you!" he said. "And thank you for keepin' it real, yo."

"Bruh, *you was my nigga when you was out here and you my nigga now... right now you need me the most, so I gotta help out... I turn my back on you, that means I'm the pussy-nigga then... and the BG bein' flaw, is something I don't believe in...*" BG quoted Plies' BID LONG. "On stacks, I love you for real, my nigga."

A lump formed in Haitian Jack's throat. He thanked God that He hadn't allowed him to kill BG. "I, I love you too, kid."

And the phone hung up. But before BG could put it down it rang again. It was the Gun Squad Click General, Pimp.

"What's good, fool?"

"Ain't shit, Pimp," BG answered. "You ready to earn the last bread I gave you?"

"Shiid, *it's all on you.*"

"Aiight, I'm 'bout to meet some niggas at the Take One to celebrate my dog's birthday. But write the address down and be ready when I get there. It'll be 'bout 1:30 if everything goes right. You feel me?"

"Yeah, gimme the info."

BG gave Pimp the address and hung up.

THE TAKE ONE LOUNGE [Two Hours Later]
BG, Var, Mane, and Rev had downed three bottles of Goose and had three more coming when Ced and Young Money arrived. They were released from the federal building two hours after BG that same night, yet this was their first time seeing each other since the holding cell. They all greeted one another and continued drinking and tipping. BG had about $80,000 in one's stacked all over the three tables that they occupied. Singles seemed to hang thick in the air like smoke above their area. All eyes were on them, because every stripper in the club was glued to their area. Fat, skinny, ugly, pretty, dime, nickel, BG didn't care, he tipped and danced them all. He was drunk as fuck and looking to get drunker. He wanted the hurt to go away.

"Waitress, bartender! One of y'all hoes! So-some-somebody get some more bottles!" BG slurred.

"Boy, you don't think you done had enough?" Var asked.

13

BG laughed and pulled out about $50,000 in crispy bank notes. "Is the money gone? Huh? We need so-som-some more mo-money?" He laughed in Var's face. "Mane! Sho-show that money! My nigga! We ain't broke! We had enough when, when, when th-the money gone, my nigga!"

Mane laughed with BG and pulled out about $30,000 in crispy *honeybees*. Besides BG, Mane was the ROC's sole survivor, and BG made damn sure he was straight. The drought was *hella bad* and birds were flying for no less than $30,000. However, BG continued to give them to Mane for $25,000. Plus BG made Mane his *right-hand,* because he'd been both loyal and efficient.

"Nigga, we rich-off-coc'! Now so-so-somebody get me some bottles!" BG demanded.

"Speakin' of money and coc', what's good, BG?" Ced asked.

"Yeah, my nigga. We kept it trill, my nigga. Lawyers cost and gettin' my Charger back, that kinda ate up some scrilla. We s'posed to be fam, but you ain't shootin' a nigga no work. What's good?" Young Money said.

BG almost fell out of his chair. "What's good? *Scared-ass-nigga!* You did what you was s'posed to do! You was eatin' off ROC product and runnin' with the ROC, but when the pressure hit you was *Mr. I Ain't With No ROC Shit*... Ced, you was there. Nigga kept callin' my muthafuckin' name like I was holdin' him in the holdin' cell... but now you ROC, huh?"

"Nah, BG, my nigga. It ain't like —"

BG cut Young Money off. "My nigga, what I owe you? You fucked up?"

"Nah, dog—"

"Nah, you cryin' like I owe you something. Here!" BG pushed about $8,000 worth of one's to him. "Is that enough? Huh?

You want a bottle, too?" BG asked and snatched an unopened bottle of Goose from Var's hand. "Here! What else you want?"

Young Money just shook his head. He felt played.

"Who else think I owe 'em? I got plenty money! I'm rich-off-coc' and I pay my way. So who else I owe?" BG said and looked at his G-shock. It was fifteen minutes to one.

Nobody said anything. Everybody just looked on as BG showed his drunk-ass.

"Now everybody quiet, huh? But y'all will be talkin' 'bout a nigga later. Wanna killa nigga like y'all did JackBoy. But guess what? Niggas ain't killin' me, 'cause I'm BG!" He stood and looked around, wobbling slightly as he stared from person to person. Everybody in the club was watching him.

Mane stood up with him.

"All this money! All these hoes! Y'all can have it! Y'all can have any hoe y'all want except for Nikkia! Because Nikkia for Haitian Jack and Haitian Jack's my muthafuckin' dog!" BG grabbed the fine stripper named Nikkia and pulled her close to him. "She for Haitian Jack! And I don't want *nann* nigga touchin' her. Fo-for-real, I don't want *nann* nigga lookin' at her no more! Mane, give her ten stacks! 'Cause she ain't strippin' no more. Give her ten stacks now and two stacks a week from now on."

Mane gave her the money and BG staggered towards the exit. He stopped when he got by the bar and turned towards the party of people he'd just left.

"Come on, Mane, follow me to the *stash-house*. I'ma give you the bricks befo' I fly out tomorrow!" He then turned and continued out.

Mane dapped Var and Rev and followed BG out of the club.

* * *

No one seemed to notice T-Zoe over in a far corner of the club. He'd been sitting there for hours watching and sipping straight shots of Seagram's Gin. He hated gin as much as he hated BG, yet because of BG it was the only liquor he could afford. It burned as it traveled down his throat. Just like his anger burned within him. BG had taken everything! He could not believe that Haitian Jack had left everything to a stinking, stupid, worthless American nigga like BG. *How could he?* T-Zoe wondered as he watched BG blow money fast. Money that he felt should have been his. T-Zoe had been so broke since Haitian Jack's arrest that he'd been getting little ounces and half-ounces thrown to him by dudes that used to work for him. Dudes [Biscayne Boyz] that were following and being served by BG.

"But I'll get you, BG, I promise you that!" T-Zoe whispered to himself.

He continued to watch a drunken BG make a fool of himself. Talking loud and throwing his money and his power around. Then BG got up and grabbed Nikkia. He said a few more foolish words and staggered off. But not before uttering the most beautiful words that T-Zoe had ever heard.

"Come on, Mane. Follow me to the *stash-house*. I'ma give you these bricks before I fly out tomorrow!"

T-Zoe couldn't believe his ears. He quickly called Stan The Man and followed BG and Mane out of the club.

AT A REMOTE WAREHOUSE LOCATION [One Hour Later]
T-Zoe sat and watched BG and Mane enter the old warehouse/ office space marked Gas & Grills by a huge yellow and red sign above its door. Mane then emerged with a large duffle bag. After placing the bag in the trunk of his car, Mane climbed in and sped off.

Where is Stan? T-Zoe wondered. He'd already called and gave him the location. "If he hurries his ass up we can empty the warehouse and kill BG all at once."

Just then he heard a car in the distance. Two vehicles with their lights out pulled beside T-Zoe's car. T-Hound, Stan The Man, and three more of their Rich Kid soldiers emerged from the mini-van and LTD.

T-Zoe got out of his car. "'Bout time," he said, greeting Stan.

"You sure this the spot?"

"Yeah!" T-Zoe explained everything from BG's drunken statement about the *stash-house* to watching Mane leave with the duffle bag. "He's still in there by himself."

"Okay." Stan The Man smiled, retrieving his pump shotgun from the LTD.

T-Hound upped her twin .45's as the other three men got AK-47's from the mini-van.

"Let's go!" Stan The Man commanded.

T-Zoe pulled his .40 caliber and followed.

Counting down from three, Stan aimed the shotgun at the dead bolt lock and fired. *BOOM!* The shotgun roared, destroying the lock. T-Hound kicked the door and it flew open. They all rushed inside, guns aimed in front of them. They had to catch BG before he realized he was being hit. Time was of the essence.

Storming through the empty office space up front, they came to the warehouse area. A line of crates, marked highly flammable, and propane tanks lined the far wall. Another set of crates and grills sat in the middle of the huge space. The crew of six spread out in hopes of finding and killing BG.

"You can hide, *you-bitch-you!* But you dyin' tonight!" Stan The Man shouted and began laughing.

A phone rung three times. Everybody paused at the sudden ringing. On the fourth ring the answering machine picked up... "Thank you for calling Gas & Grills. We're out, please leave a message," the machine beeped and BG's voice could be heard. "T-Zoe, I wish I could see yo' *stupid-ass* face, *bitch-nigga!* I'm glad you brought Stan and T-Hound, 'cause this for Barbie, LG, Pretty Boy and Fats!"

The message ended and a long beep sounded, *beeeeeeeeep!*

"Aaaaahhhhhh, fuck!" T-Hound yelled and ran as the bright orange, blue, and red lights seemed to erupt from everywhere. The boom was so loud that it went unheard by those within the wave of glowing pressure and incinerating heat.

The entire warehouse went up in a rumbling, earth-shaking blaze, killing everyone inside.

ONE-HUNDRED YARDS AWAY

BG sat holding the cell phone as he watched through binoculars. The orange, white, and yellow glow seemed to appear out of nowhere and consume the entire building all at once. Even from one-hundred yards away the ground shook beneath the cargo van that they were in.

"Gotdamn, Pimp!" BG exclaimed. "Fuck you put in there, yo?"

"Enough," Pimp said, holding the detonating device. "Now let's get the fuck outta here!"

"Yeah, hell yeah!" Mane yelled and got out of the van. He'd never expected anything like this when he'd left out of the warehouse earlier and circled around the block to pick BG up just as he'd squeezed through a rear window of the warehouse.

BG dapped Pimp up and thanked him. "Bet that up, boy."

"No problem, man, holla if you need me."

BG hopped out of the van and jumped in with Mane. The two drove off laughing.

"My nigga, you're a better actor than that cracka that played Scarface," Mane said. "I really thought you was drunk."

"Oh, I was feelin' it, but I chewed two X-pills before I got there. My dog said you can't get drunk off them shits," BG stated. "But a nigga feel crazy! I'm 'bout to go home, suck Monique's pussy and put that *pound-game* down! You hear me, *bob*?"

Mane bussed up laughing. "Big homie, you a fool!"

Chapter 2

TWENTY-FOUR MONTHS LATER

BG and Mane were sitting in their traphouse on 58th Street and 6th Avenue. They'd just closed shop. Two duffle bags of drug money sat next to the coffee table. An AR-15 and a Glock 19 sat on top of the coffee table. Business was booming, because BG's ROC GANG seemed to be the only gang in the city that kept dope consistently. And with all of the traps that they had established, BG had stopped selling weight. All of the ROC traps and the spots that the Biscayne Boyz held sold nothing but *nickel rocks* and *eightballs* of crack.

"Boy, we're some rich niggas," Mane said, hitting the blunt of 'dro and passing it to BG.

BG nodded. Hit the weed hard. They'd done it. The city was theirs. "Yeah, lil' nigga, we're the richest niggas in Dade or Broward County... And we did it off cocaine."

The two laughed and smoked.

Mane was about to take the *seven-gram* blunt of 'dro back from BG when something exploded and the trap's front door flew off of its hinges.

"What the fuck?!" BG yelled and grabbed the Glock 19.

Mane grabbed the AR-15 and chambered it just as the first person ran through the door. Mane did not hesitate one second, he let loose. *Yaaaaaaaaaaaaaaaaak!* Hitting the man and the two men behind him with about forty rounds of .223's.

Another explosion sounded. A bright light flashed and the living room filled with smoke.

"F.B.I! Drop your weapons and get down!" BG heard someone yell just as Mane took a chestful of lead and went down firing his weapon.

"Maaaaane!" BG screamed and began bussing his Glock wildly.

Tat! Tat! Tat! Tat! Tat! Tat! he fired, killing two more officers. Tears ran down his dark brown face, from the tear gas and the emotions stirred by Mane's death. BG covered his nose with the neck of his shirt and ran for the back door. He fired two shots through the door before opening it. Stepping over the dead policemen, BG ran and hit the back fence. His BMW 750Li was parked on the next block. BG jumped in and punched it down the block.

As soon as he cleared the street two unmarked police cars jumped on his trail. *Damn!* BG cursed, sweat covering his face. His heart about to beat out of his chest. He zig-zagged through back streets until he caught an on ramp to I-95 North. The speedometer read 120 mph. Yet the two police cars were still on him. *If I make it outta this shit I gotta get that Gallardo!* he thought as he hit the 95th Street exit and blew through the red light. Horns blew loudly and people swerved to avoid colliding with the speeding BMW.

Running the light on 7th Avenue, Westbound, BG kept his foot in the tank. Pastor Troy's *No More Play In GA* blasted through the car's sound system. BG snatched the wheel, cutting dangerously across oncoming traffic. He was now southbound on Little River Drive. He ran every stop sign on the long street and came past the new park doing 70 mph. Praying to God that there was no traffic on 79th Street, BG fishtailed onto the main thoroughfare and punched it hard. The BMW was performing, yet somehow the police were still hot on his ass.

What kind of engines do they have in those ugly-ass police cars?! he wondered.

Boom! An explosion sounded and the car dipped on the front passenger side.

BG fought with the wheel. A loud grinding sound could be heard as sparks flew from beneath the car. The tire had bussed or been shot. BG slammed on the brakes and jumped out firing the Mac-90 that had been laying on the backseat.

Yak! Yak! Yak! Yak! Yak! he got off, hitting both officers in the first car and causing the second car to slam on brakes.

Boom! Boom! Boom! Boom! Boom! the officer on the passenger side fired.

BG ducked behind the BMW. He waited eight seconds before peeking around the car's fender. *Oh shit!* he thought. It was Agent Gomez. BG took a deep breath and came up firing. *Yak! Yak! Yak! Yak! Yak! Yak!* Agent Gomez dove for cover and BG took off running.

He jumped two fences and came out behind a store. There was a group of men standing around shooting dice and drinking. They were all wearing red. As he got closer BG recognized two of the men. They locked eyes. *Ooooh, shit!* BG thought as he shouldered the Mac-90 and let off about ten rounds. *Yaaaaaaaaaak!*

Leroy Bethal and Bulldog dove to the ground.

BG kept running. He could faintly hear footfall behind him. He held the rifle and ran as fast as he could. Taking fences and running through yards with big barking dogs, BG made it back to 79th and saw no one. He had lost them. *Thank God!* he said to himself and jogged off. He needed to get off of the street and call for a ride. There was a small storefront church sitting there on 79th Street and 20th Avenue. BG tossed the AR-15 and ducked inside.

"Good day, brutha," a middle-aged man in suit and tie greeted him.

"Go… good… day… to you… brutha," BG gasped, wiping sweat from his face. He was tired as hell.

The man looked at BG. Furrowed his brow. "Brutha, are you okay? Is something wrong?"

BG shook his head no.

The man nodded and allowed BG to go on inside. There were about seventy people inside. Men, women, and children of different ages. BG found himself a seat in the middle and slouched down in his seat. He needed to rest and catch his breath.

"Look to the person beside you. Shake their hand and tell them, *peace be onto you*," the speaker said. BG and the female exchanged the greeting. "Look them in the eyes and tell them *there's one amongst you that loves you*."

Again, BG and the girl repeated what the speaker had said. Only then did BG look up at the rostrum and see that the speaker was a woman. She had her black hair flat-wrapped. Her eyes were big and intelligent – lively. She had very big lips and dark-brown skin. The business skirt and jacket that she wore was tailored to perfection, accenting her small waist and wide hips. The chick had body. But gazing above her 34-B's, he saw that she did not possess traditional beauty.

"Have you all not heard that we should love our bruthas and sistas and want for them that which we want for ourselves? This is scripture. And scripture is indeed God's word. Am I right bruthas and sistas? But you're not thinking about God when you're dealing and killing! Our people's blood is *all on you*."

The people in attendance all nodded their heads and recited their *amen's*.

BG just sat there, wondering what the hell he was doing in here.

As if reading his mind, the speaker said, "I'll answer that in a minute, but right now, by a show of hands, how many of y'all believe in God?"

Everybody raised their hand except for BG. He believed, but wasn't sure of what he believed. The streets had really hardened him. Confused him. He'd seen and done so much, he was not sure if he had a right to claim his belief in God. After all, the things that he did for a living was evil... *And it's all on me*, he knew.

"Okay, by a show of hands, how many of you love black people?" the unattractive woman asked.

Again, everybody raised their hands except for BG. Everybody he'd ever killed, ordered to be killed, or sold harmful drugs to were black. He thought he loved black people, but something inside of him told him that *you don't do those kinds of things to people you love.*

The speaker fixed those big eyes of hers on BG and said, "Brutha, I know that you're confused and hurting. And even though you have lots of money and power and friends, you're lonely. Brutha, you're here because that small voice, the God in you, it just won't let you rest..." She paused, her big lips frozen in a smile. Moistening them with her tongue, she continued. "In the vilest of men, there rests the spirt of God. That still small voice is everlasting goodness, because man is made up of that God spirit, the soul, which is mind and body."

BG nodded, though he was mightily confused. *How does this bitch know what I'm thinking?!*

"The mind is the free will that God gave man, which causes man to sin. It's the mind, your free will, and the spirit, God in man, that's always in continuous conflict! Every time you pick up that gun, leave the house to cheat on the woman that loves you, that still small voice, God in man, will tell you, *man, I wouldn't do that if I was you*. But the sinful mind of man, that free will, the greedy and lustful self, it'll step right in and say, *man, it's all good*. This will go on for as long as the spirit will allow. That spirit is the only thing that makes man redeemable... So, brutha, once that spirit, God Himself in you, decides it's had enough and exits the building, man, on this plane, ceases to exist!"

But what I'm s'posed to do? Niggas tryna kill me! My brutha gone... BG thought.

"Oh, man," she said sadly. "I've heard thy voice and I was afraid: Oh Lord, revive they work in the midst of the years... in the midst of years He made known, in wrath remember mercy... Lord, God, forgive my poor brutha, wash him in the blood and forgive him. For ignorance and want have destroyed him and the entire generation that he came with..."

BG saw tears in her eyes.

The girl beside him was crying also.

BG looked around and saw that everybody was crying. That's when he saw them. Agent Gomez, Leroy Bethal, and Bulldog were all standing at the rear of the small church. They all had their guns drawn.

Gomez smiled broadly. "Looks like this is it, BG."

"And you couldn't have picked a better place to go," Leroy Bethal said.

Bulldog nodded and cocked his gun.

BG stood up.

"You wanna say a prayer before meetin' your maker?"

BG didn't say anything. He just eyed them. It was time to pay for all of the wrong he'd done. *And I'm not scared... When I go, it'll be on both feet, never knees in dirt!* he thought to himself and thanked God for both the gift of life and the curse of death.

Leroy Bethal shrugged. "No prayer? Well, *it's all on you,*" he said before aiming and firing.

Boom! Boom! Boom! Boom! Bulldog and Agent Gomez fired along with Leroy Bethal.

BG closed his eyes and anticipated the impact of the hot slugs... But they never came.

BG opened his eyes and saw that the three men were firing on the members of the church. The men, women, and children were running and ducking to no avail. The three evil murderers were cutting the innocent people down like dogs. Blood was everywhere. Their screams were deafening.

"Nooooo!" BG screamed.

The three men laughed as they continued firing.

BG looked and saw that the speaker had been shot. He ran to her. Drew here into his arms. Blood ran out of her mouth, over her thick lips. Her big eyes stared into his. He held her. Hugged her body to his. She was no longer ugly to him. She was dying. She was beautiful. Her blood was all over his clothes... *On his hands.*

"I'm sorry," BG told her.

She smiled. "Choices... Free will, BG... *It's all on you,*" she said and died in his arms.

"No... No, don't die... Don't die," BG cried, his whole body convulsing, shaking... He felt hands grabbing him, pulling him, shaking him. He heard his name being called.

"BG! BG! Boy, get up! You're dreamin'!"

BG snatched away and quickly sat up. He looked around the room. There were no dead people. No blood. Monique sat beside him in bed. There was no Agent Gomez, Leroy Bethal, or Bulldog. BG closed his eyes and shook his head.

"Baby, are you aiight?" Monique asked, rubbing his sweaty face with her soft hand.

He nodded. "Yeah, I'm aiight." He reached in his nightstand drawer and pulled out a fifth of aged Bourbon. The fine whiskey was reddish in color. It went down smoothly. BG downed a third of it before re-corking the crystal bottle.

Monique shook her head sadly. She felt so bad for him. Every night demons plagued his sleep. The streets were destroying him slowly but surely. A tear escaped her eye as she watched him get out of bed and begin dressing. "BG, baby, where are you goin'?"

"To check a few traps, baby," BG said and went in the bathroom.

He was in the bathroom for fifteen minutes before he came out and exited their master bedroom. He had to get out and move around – breathe. But before leaving the house he stopped in the nursery and checked on his one-year-old son, LG. He was the absolute light of BG's life. A gift from Monique and God. BG smiled down at his son. He had a headful of hair and eyes like his mother.

"At least one of us can sleep," he said, hoping that his son never had to go through what he'd been through in life.

Exiting that room, he checked in on Devon, who was also sleeping soundly. Devon was his little man and BG wanted the best for him.

Satisfied that his family was good, BG tucked his .40 caliber and stepped out into the real world, where it was strictly *get it how you live*...

Chapter 3

It was still dark outside when BG pulled the slick silver BMW 760Li out of the big six car garage and drove through the electric gate that surrounded his eight bedroom modern ranch-style home. He'd sold Haitian Jack's house as well as Monique's house. The stakes were too high now and he couldn't risk having anyone know where him and his family rested their heads.

Driving east through Hialeah on 103rd Street, BG lit one of the pre-rolled blunts that he kept on him at all times. He inhaled it deeply, savoring the fruity taste of the exotic haze. It was exactly what he needed. Thoughts of the nightmare he'd had last night played at his mind. It was so vivid. So graphic and daunting. *A revelation?* BG wondered was the dream forewarning or determining? Had the die been casted or did he still have time? So much was unclear. The woman with the big eyes and thick lips? A queer sensation washed over him. BG didn't know if it was a feeling of guilt or want. Subconsciously he looked at his hands and shirt, expecting to see her blood. He felt his heart rate quicken just as it had in the dream… *But the sinful mind of man, that free will, the greedy and lustful self, it'll tell you that everything's okay… But it's not! The blood of your people, their suffering and deaths, the next generation that we'll lose to your example, is all on you!* he remembered her saying. BG hit the blunt again and tried to forget. But he knew that he would never forget that woman's face or her words.

Floating through Miami Shores, BG slowly circled the block of 118th Street twice before parking at the split-level dwelling that he'd recently purchased. Briefcase in hand, he got out and went in the house. The living room was nicely furnished and the kitchen was well stocked. There was thick carpet, some leather bean bags, and a 72" flat-screen TV in the den. Other than that, the house was empty. BG grabbed a bottle of orange juice out of the fridge and went upstairs. He went to the master bedroom. Stacked along the walls were cardboard boxes. There were twenty boxes in all. Each contained $375,000, $7,500,000 in total.

BG stared at the boxes. He knew that he had to hurry up and do something with the money before something crazy happened. So far he'd managed to launder about $2,000,000 through Monique's hair salons, but he knew that he couldn't keep doing it that way. The process was too long and the cost was too high. *And I still got 300 birds left,* he thought to himself.

Closing the bedroom door, BG went downstairs and out of the front door. He jumped back in the BMW and drove off. Jay-Z's *Lucky Me* played as he rode. It was his new favorite song, his anthem. BG often put the song on repeat and just rode out. The words were so real. They reflected his life. He'd made it, but simply could not enjoy his success. *Yeah*, BG thought, *lucky me.*

His next stop was in El Portel, where he had a three bedroom house on 93rd Street and 1st Avenue. This house was sparsely furnished. Just the bare necessities. BG went into the master bedroom. Again there were cardboard boxes along the wall, fifteen in all. Each box held twenty tightly wrapped kilos of cocaine. The last of 650 kilos that he'd hit for. As he stared at the boxes he saw the faces of Missy, Jackboy, Bo-Jit, Hot Rod, Lil 50, Pretty Boy, France, Stanka, Fats, Black Barbie, and his brother, LG. They'd all lost their lives behind this shit. But he was still here to deal with the backlash and frustration of life without the people he loved. BG shook his head, *lucky me.*

* * *

Back in the sleek luxury sports car, behind dark tinted windows, BG rode around aimlessly. Troubled, though he had no immediate problems. Just a lot of money. A lot of drugs. Responsibility. Absentmindedly, he shrugged his shoulders, as if confessing to himself that he really didn't know... *To know?* he thought, knowing that the truth was, *It was too early to tell, because means could only be assessed in relation to the ends.* His phone rung. It was Nikkia, Haitian Jack's woman.

"Talk to me," he answered, happy to have escaped his thoughts for a minute.

"Hey, baby," Nikkia sang happily. "How are you today?"

"I'm makin' it, ma. What's got you so happy today?"

"My man," Nikkia sang. "I just got back in last night from visitin' him."

"Okay, how's he doin'?"

"He's doin' good." Nikkia paused for a moment. "BG, he kind of needs your help."

"Nikkia, don't play with me!" BG checked her. "You know I'll do *anything* for Jack."

"Well." She sighed heavily. "We need to talk."

"When?"

"Soon as possible."

"I have a few stops to make, but I can be over there around six o'clock."

"That'll be cool, BG."

"Aiight, ma, see you then."

Nikkia blew a kiss over the phone and hung up.

BC continued driving. He was now near 7th Avenue and decided to slide through his old hood, Little Haiti. He always made it his business to stop through at least once a week. Aside from a few small children running around, 58th was empty. BG circled and made his way up to the corner store. He saw his old Haitian friend, Mr. Fee, sitting beside the store on a crate. The hot sun baking his black skin. BG parked and got out.

Before going over to sit with Mr. Fee, BG went inside of the store and bought three Jamaican beef patties and two pints of Wild Irish Rose. He then pulled up a crate beside the old Haitian man and handed him a brown paper bag.

"BG," Mr. Fee said, taking the bag.

"What's up, Mr. Fee?"

The old man hunched his skinny shoulders and looked in the bag. A frown appeared on his dark, shiny face. "Where's my stuff?"

Eating a Jamaican patty, BG said, "It's right here. But you're not gettin' it 'til you eat those two patties."

Mr. Fee sighed and started eating.

BG watched him eat. He knew that Mr. Fee probably had not eaten in a day or two. All the old man wanted to do was drink. Nothing else seemed to matter to him. His clothes were old and dirty. His hair and beard were matted and smelly. Mr. Fee probably had not bathed or slept in a clean bed in over a year. Yet for some reason beyond his own perception, BG had grown to favor the man. Whenever he visited the hood he made it his business to spend some time with Mr. Fee.

"Okay, BG," Mr. Fee said, showing BG the empty paper bag. The two beef patties were gone.

"Damn, you was kind of hungry, huh?" BG asked.

"No. I thirsty."

BG laughed before opening one of the pints and pouring some on the ground. He then drunk some and passed the cold bottle of cheap wine to Mr. Fee.

Taking the wine, Mr. Fee swallowed deeply, nearly emptying it, and then asked BG, "You always pour out, on ground, why?"

"Shiid, for the homies that's gone."

Mr. Fee shook his head. "No," he said. "If friends are good like you, no ground. They fly with the clouds. So next one, throw it up."

BG smiled. It donned on him that Jay-Z had said almost the exact same words on *Lucky Me*. "You got that, Mr. Fee, from now on we're gonna *throw it up*."

Opening the second pint, BG swigged and passed it.

Mr. Fee drunk the sweet wine like it was water. Leaving just enough to wet BG's whistles, he passed it back.

"Mr. Fee, man, why do you do this?"

He hunched his little shoulders. "Nothin' else to do. Wife leave. Children grow up and live their life... I lived my life."

"But like this? I mean, are you happy?"

Again the old man shrugged. "What you do, are you happy? Lot of money, lot of problems. You are the same like me. Not happy, but livin' your life." Mr. Fee pointed to his head. "Right here make us happy. Not where you live or what you have. No. It is what you know, what you think, that make you happy or not."

BG nodded. "Yeah, it's all on me, huh?"

Mr. Fee nodded his agreement.

"Thanks, Mr. Fee." BG handed the old man $200 and jumped back in the BMW, northbound.

Chapter 4

Danielle woke up to the bright Miami sun shining through the bedroom window of her new home in Hollywood, Florida. It was a gift to her and Gemo from BG. She absolutely loved the four bedroom, four bath house with the sunken den and screened patio.

Looking beside her in the big king-sized bed, Danielle saw that Gemo was still laying sleep. She sucked her teeth and hit him upside the head. "Gemo, boy, you better get up!"

Gemo looked at her and yawned. He'd been out of federal prison for about sixteen months now. "Danielle, what have I told your ass about botherin' me when I'm sleep?"

Danielle laughed, her big double-D's bouncing as she did so. "Boy, you better get up. You know you're s'posed to be at the bar, Gemo."

"Fuck that bar."

"No, get up, Gemo!" she said loudly, shaking him.

"Aiight, aiight, damn!" Gemo got up and tumbled off into the bathroom. He hated that damn bar. Every day, the same people came in talking the same nonsense and ordered the same damn things. He'd been working in Wet Wetz since the day he was released from the halfway house. *And goddamn it, it's time to get it how I live!* he thought as he exited the bathroom.

Danielle stood naked, waiting to get in the bathroom. She'd put on a few pounds since he'd been gone, but she was still fine as hell in his book. Every night it seemed that they made love until the sun came up. And still, Gemo never got tired of her. His time away had taught him to appreciate her. And being that he'd lost Black Barbie, Gemo did not have the time or energy to start anything new. No, he was home, and home was with Danielle.

Dressing in brown dress slacks, a beige silk shirt, and brown big block gators, Gemo brushed his low fade and his big beard before calling out to Danielle, "Baby, I'm gone!"

"Okay, baby, love you!" Danielle yelled from the shower.

Gemo pocketed a knot of twenty and fifty dollar bills, four pre-rolled blunts of purple, and exited the house.

The sun was summer time hot as he climbed into the dark-gray Range Rover that he'd just recently bought. It was his coming home present to himself. He loved the sleek new SUV. Pulling it out of the yard, Gemo fired up a blunt and sped off of the block. Bobby Womack's *Only Survivor* played as he rode along. He'd first heard the song in prison. And as he listened to it now, he almost shed a tear, remembering all of the good men he'd left behind those prison walls. Men that he loved. Men that had helped him through his bid... Men, he knew, that were never coming home. *Damn,* Gemo thought, feeling the purple lifting him to that magical place. *To lose your life to the system, for something you did as a means to survive, that was a hard lesson*, Gemo mused. He knew that he had to be careful, because the feds and the rats that worked with them would love nothing more than to stick him with a long sentence. *Nah, I'm not goin' back to prison*, he promised himself. Because he was not just *getting it how he lived* for himself, he was doing it for all of the soldiers that were stuck behind enemy lines and could not get it for themselves.

Before going to the bar, where he knew he'd be stuck for the rest of the day, Gemo decided to go through the old neighborhood. He needed to holla at his main man King. The two had done a lot of business together in the past. *I hope this damn nigga is out here*, Gemo said to himself.

As he bent the corner of 57th Street and 6th Avenue, he spotted King's forest-green BMW 750Li. Gemo parked his Range Rover in front of it and hopped out. King was sitting in the car with a fine-ass Haitian chick that Gemo used to mess with.

"What's up, boy?" he greeted King.

Smiling, King jumped out of the car and hugged Gemo. "What they do, boy?"

"Ain't nothin', fool. I see you're still on them *thots*," he stated, nodding his head towards the thick Haitian girl sitting in King's BMW.

King laughed, his long dreadlocks swinging as he shook his head. "Just makin' the rounds and shorty is really good company. You feel me?"

"Yeah, fool, you know I feel you." The two laughed some more.

As they stood talking beside Gemo's Range Rover, Gemo could not help but notice the steady stream of customers shopping at King's trap. They were coming and going with great frequency.

Gemo looked at the tall, skinny Haitian standing in front of him, mouthful of gold-teeth and skin as black as tar, and for a minute he could not understand anything the man was saying. He heard cash registers and money machines. "Aye, I don't mean to cut you off, because that's some real shit you're sayin'." Gemo couldn't have told that man what he'd just said to save his life, because he hadn't been listening. "But, yo, what're you pumpin' outta there?"

"Dozier."

"What the fuck is that?"

"A speed-ball. Heroin and cocaine mixed. I put one gram of boy on every two grams of that girl... No cut! I keep that thang raw... You feel me? Nothin' but quarter and hun'ed dollar pieces."

Gemo nodded. That was nice money. "What are you coppin'?"

"Half-a-brick of 'roin, a brick of coc'... But, dog, they're killin' me on the coc'! They whackin' the shit and taxin' me!" King eyed Gemo. "You can't get nothin'?"

Gemo shook his head. "I don't know." He'd been trying to get some work out of BG for the past six months. Every time BG would come up with some bullshit and shoot him some money.

"Fuck you mean? Your lil' cousin got it all."

"So why you won't fuck with him?"

"'Cause, fool ain't fuckin' with niggas." King thought for a minute. "Look, fool, I can get that 'roin all day. You get that coc' and we'll take off!"

"Aiight, that's all I needed to hear. I'm on it, fool."

The two dapped each other up and went their separate ways...

Chapter 5

Tony Galletta was a big man. Standing at six-foot-three-inches, 305 pounds, not too many people dared to get in the big Italian's way. He had a thick black mop of hair on his square head. His face always shaved clean. Anybody looking at Tony Galletta or spending any length of time around him would swear by God that he was a mafia don or capo. While in actuality he was the furthest thing from it. The giant Italian with the foul mouth and great tan was the head coordinating detective in the major crimes division and the regional director of PALS – the police athletic league. At age 44, Tony had spent 23 years on the force. And besides his wife and beautiful daughter, his career was his life.

"Tony!" his small wife yelled from the kitchen. Anne Galletta was always loud and talked a mile a minute. Her long black hair was heavily streaked with gray, and at age 38 Anne looked older than her 44 year old husband. "Tony, are you eatin' before you leave?"

"No, honey, I'll grab somethin' at the bar!" Tony replied.

"Okay, say hello to the guys for me!"

"Alright, honey!" Tony yelled and made his way to the front door of the family's split-level three bedroom home. He'd purchased the home in Pembroke Pines two years ago, a month after buying his brand-new Cadillac CTS. "Angelina, damn it, you'd better move your skinny-ass if you wanna ride to the fuckin' bar, goddamn it!"

"Dad!" Angelina yelled through the house. "I'm comin'!"

"Well fuckin' come on, will you?!"

"Tony!" Anne screamed from the kitchen. "Why do you have to talk to the girl like that?!"

"Because she's fuckin' holdin' me up!" Tony was pissed now. He paid all of the bills. Risked his life every day for the sake of his family and the overall goodwill of the community, but his wife always took their daughter's side. "And goddamn it, I'm leavin' her!"

"Daaaaad! I'm comin'!" Angelina screamed as she came running down the stairs.

Tony's eyes bucked when he saw his 18-year-old daughter. *Holy mother of Jesus?!* he said to himself. "Angelina, sweetheart, you look like a goddamn hooker!"

"Daddy!" the sexy 18-year-old yelled and stomped her silver six-inch heel on the tiled floor. Angelina was exactly five-foot-ten-inches tall, 115 pounds. Her long black hair hung past her shoulders. Creamy white skin, regal nose, and dark-brown eyes. With measurements of 38D-26-28, Angelina was built like your typical white girl – sexy, but not quite fine.

"Could you get those little shorts and that little bra *thingy* any tighter? For Christ sakes!?"

By now Anne had come out of the kitchen to see what all the fuss was about. Seeing Angelina in the little pink satin booty-shorts and the tight halter top, she gasped. "Honey, my God, you look like one of those black video girls."

Angelina sucked her teeth. "Mom, this is the style."

"Then they'll be burying you in style if you don't go and take that shit off!" Tony yelled. His big square face was red with anger.

"Moooooom?" Angelina whined.

"No, sweetheart, your father's right this time... Your outfit's a bit much," Anne whispered, wondering how on earth did Angelina manage to squeeze into the tiny shorts and halter top.

"Aaaagghh, you guys are so... old!" Angelina yelled and stomped off.

"Kids," Tony said.

"Yeah, kids," his wife repeated.

Five minutes later, Angelina came back down the stairs wearing tight blue jeans and a T-shirt.

Tony nodded his approval and he and his daughter left.

Chapter 6

As soon as the big booty chick got up off of her bed and went in the bathroom, Mane wiped his dick off on her sheets and quickly got dressed. He was slipping his One's on when she came back into the room carrying a towel.

After sucking her teeth, she said, "Damn, Mane, you just gon' clear it like that?"

That's normally what I do after I get what I want, he thought, but replied, "I gotta handle some business right quick."

When Mane stood up she walked up on him, rubbing her naked body against his. "So, umm, when a female gon' see you again?"

"Shiid, probably when you get paid," Mane answered her.

"When I get paid?!"

"Yeah."

"Boy, I ain't got no damn job," she stated, her pretty face balled up in a frown.

"Then." Mane shrugged his young shoulders. "You probably won't be seein' me."

"Ut'un!" She sucked her teeth and struck a pose. "Nigga, no the fuck you didn't!"

"Yeah, I did, lil' momma, but you shouldn't have." Mane laughed.

"Oh, so shit funny after you done fucked. Now you wanna play a female?!"

"Ain't that what you was tryna do to me?"

"And how you figure that?" She had the beginning of a tear in her eye.

"Before BG put me on, when I was ridin' a bike, before the Lambo; shorty, you wasn't checkin' for me."

"So that's how you feel?!"

"Ma, that's how it is. My hoe gotta be 'bout me and she gotta have somethin'."

She nodded. Wiped her eyes. "Okay, when I get somethin', then what?!"

"Then we'll talk some more," Mane said and left. He'd been trying to sex shorty for a week. Now his mission was complete – *on to the next one.*

Mane laughed to himself as he fired up the powerful engine in the Lamborghini and peeled out down the street. Yo Gotti's *They Know* played as he shifted gears and blew by cars. People could not help but to jock him when they saw him in the $270,000 car. In the thirty days that he'd had the car, Mane had fucked more chicks than he'd fucked in the entire twenty years he'd been on this earth.

He looked at his gold Rolex. It was one o'clock. *Damn,* he cursed himself. *Fuckin' with that bitch!* He was supposed to meet BG at Wet Wetz an hour ago. He had the $125,000 that he owed BG in the trunk. *And I ain't got but a half-bird left,* Mane thought and punched it. He could not miss BG because he needed more dope for the traps. *You're bullshittin', Mane! You gotta get it how you live, boy!* he told himself and hoped to God that BG was still at Wet Wetz when he got there...

Chapter 7

Gemo stood behind the large glass bar, wiping its surface and toweling out glasses. The bar took up the entire back wall of the spacious social club. Behind the bar was the large kitchen. BG had spent $750,000 gutting and remodeling the space that had once been Club Rendezvous in Miami Lakes, right off Main Street. Every booth, table and chair was made of thick glass and steel. The walls were covered with abstract paintings and 72" flat-screens. Upstairs was an adult game room: pool tables, a variety of large screen shooting and driving games, and rows of slot machines. The food and drinks were good, everything was upscale. Even the topless waitresses – a variety of pretty white girls with large breasts, long legs, and no ass. Very few black people patronized Wet Wetz, however, the few that did had plenty money.

It was exactly one o'clock, right after the lunch time rush, happy hour. It was their busiest time of day. The corporate movers and shakers came in to get away from their offices and politick while enjoying the fine foods, drinks, and topless chicks. Soft jazz and boring elevator music played. The atmosphere was perfect for negotiating million dollar business deals. So Wet Wetz also attracted its share of underworld bosses. BG's marketing concept had created the ideal melting pot.

Gemo had only been behind the bar for an hour, having arrived at twelve o'clock, and had already served over 50 drinks.

On a bad day he took home $200 in tips, not to mention BG paid him $1,500 a week. The situation was legitimate, the job was easy, and the money was damn good. Anybody would be happy to have been placed in Gemo's position, anybody but Gemo. He hated standing behind the bar, serving people. Every day he fought to stay his course and ignore the call of the streets. *Hustling.* Politicking with bosses and making moves was embedded in his DNA. So it was difficult to exist in such an atmosphere and not be a part of it. It was even harder to watch BG, his little cousin, someone he had raised, take center stage. People came in, both black and white, male and female, and waited their turn to hold counsel with BG. Yet all they wanted from him was a damn drink. *Nah, fuck this shit! I gotta get back in the mix. I can't be workin' for this nigga! I've lost Barbie, lost seven years of my life, and I'll be damned if I lose who I am! I'm Get Money, the get it how you live icon... I gotta maintain that! It ain't on BG, it's all on me*, Gemo thought to himself. But the first thing he had to do was get BG to give him some cocaine for King's dope spot. He was pondering this when Andras Simonyi, two of his young soldiers, and a Spanish gentlemen that Gemo had never seen before all walked in together, taking up seats at the end of the long bar, away from everyone. Andras and the Spanish man sat. Andras' two goons stood four paces back.

Gemo and Andras had become friendly over the past year. The pale Hungarian was a sports fanatic and loved the Miami Heat and the Miami Dolphins with a passion. He also loved the bar's imported *Black Label* vodka. BG's supplier got him the exclusive clear liquor for $187 a fifth, so Wet Wetz was one of three places in Dade County that carried it.

Andras came in every day, usually around one o'clock, to talk about the Heat or Dolphins, take a meeting or two with his associates, and enjoy the relaxed social setting. And every day he ordered a platter of fried goose liver sandwiches and a bottle of *Black Label*, which the house sold for $300 a bottle or $20 a shot.

Gemo had heard whispers that Andras was supposed to be somebody in his Hungarian circle. Skinny, soft-spoken, about five-foot-nine-inches in height, he didn't look like anybody important to Gemo. He always wore slacks, soft leather shoes, and silk long sleeve shirts – always untucked. And he always had the same two young Hungarian men with him. No, he did not look like much to Gemo, though he tipped good and seemed to be a real down to earth guy.

Making his way over to where Andras and his associate was seated, Gemo placed two glasses of ice in front of them and cracked the seal on a fresh bottle of *Black Label*. He poured both men three fingers and sat the bottle down.

"Thanks, Gemo," Andras said and continued talking to the man he'd walked in with.

Gemo turned and saw that the nerdy white man that had been sitting with BG for the last hour was now gathering his things to leave. After calling over someone to man the bar, Gemo took off for his cousin's table before somebody else walked up.

"Damn, lil' cuz, what it do?" Gemo said, sliding in the booth with BG.

BG looked at his big cousin and smiled brightly. He was happy to see him out of prison and doing good for himself. Gemo had showed him so much when they were growing up. Now it felt good to him to be in a position to provide for his big cousin. "Shiid, cuz, it's doin' what it's s'posed to do. You dig?"

Gemo nodded. Eyed his little cousin. He no longer wore the big beard like Gemo. BG was becoming, or had become, his own man. Gemo liked that, but something inside of him also resented it. Most likely it was that same something that blamed BG for Black Barbie and LG's death.

BG sensed that something was on his cousin's mind. "Gemo, cuz, what's up? You lookin' like you're goin' through it 'bout something."

"I am, cuz," Gemo said and sighed loudly. "I need you, BG...
I mean, I really need you, cuz."

"Whatever, talk to me."

"I've been out 'bout a year and a half, doin' what you've
asked me to, and I 'preciate everything that you've set out for me,
but this ain't me, BG."

"What do you mean?" BG's face wrinkled with concern.
"You need some bread?"

"Nah, cuz, I need my own! Standin' behind that bar every
day is killin' me." Gemo's eyes were sad.

"I feel you, cuz, and I'm puttin' something together right
now. That cracka that just left is my accountant. We're tryna work
something so that I can spend another mill' or two, open up
something big. Wet Wetz is doin' good, we wanna open up a strip
club, something big, with the Wet Wetz's name on it. You can —"

"Nah." Gemo waved his hand, cutting BG off. "I don't wanna
run a strip club for you."

"Then what do you want?"

"What I've been askin' you for the past six months!"

BG shook his head sadly. "Cuz, come on, man."

"Come on, what?! BG, I'm a grown-ass man, older than you
and Danielle. And, cuz, I can't keep lettin' y'all dictate my moves.
I'm a street nigga! I was in the streets when Danielle met me and I
was out there before you decided to step off the porch. It's in me,
cuz! And I want, no, I *need* to get back to it."

"Gemo, I thought we already went through this. I can't do
what you're askin' me to do," BG said sadly. It pained him to have
to tell Gemo no.

"Oh, you can't plug me but you can feed the lil' nigga
Mane?!"

"Nah, cuz, I owe Mane. That lil' nigga was here when I built
this ROC shit."

"And you don't owe me?! I didn't help you build this?!" Gemo stared at BG. "If I wouldn't have plugged you with my connect, ZoeMan, and you wouldn't have robbed and killed him, you wouldn't be sittin' so tight and I wouldn't be askin' you for shit, because I would have a plug."

BG shook his head. "Nah, cuz, I didn't rob and kill ZoeMan."

Gemo laughed. "So he killed himself and gave you over 500 kilos?!"

"Cuz, ZoeMan tried to kill me! He jumped out there and I bussed his ass! Like I'll do any nigga that steps 'cross that line." BG found himself getting upset.

"So what're you sayin', lil' cuz?"

"I'm sayin' I did what I had to do, cuz. I didn't want none of that shit to happen. Everything that I've been doin' is to better our situation. You have to trust me on this, cuz. I got 300 bricks left. Me and Jack decided that we'd break it all down since we already got the traps to push it through. Once that's gone, that's it, cuz, we're out. Game's over. But you have to trust a nigga –"

"Like I trusted you with Barbie?"

"What?!"

"You heard me! I trusted you with Barbie and she's dead. I trusted you with my plug and you robbed and killed him! I've lost everything, cuz, and you keep talkin' this trust shit, but I don't even know where you live at, cuz," Gemo said angrily.

BG could not figure out where all of this was coming from. They'd already talked about the circumstances surrounding Black Barbie's death. He'd already apologized for that. He'd also bought Gemo a new house and gave him $250,000 when he'd gotten out of the halfway house. "Cuz, what does knowin' where I stay have to do with any of this? If you don't live there and you're not tryna rob or kill me, then my address is useless information."

"You know where I stay."

"Then maybe you need to sell the house and move, because you're trippin'."

Gemo was about to say something real disrespectful, but he caught himself. Thought a second. He loved his little cousin, but he was not feeling him. "Look, BG, this shit is goin' somewhere else. I apologize if I came off fucked up, but I'ma get me some work... I'd prefer it be with you, cuz, I wanna fuck with you. Like it used to be. But if you ain't really tryna eat with me, I'll just have to mob with somebody else... And just know this, either way, I'm finished with this bartendin' shit." His expression was solemn. "It's all on you."

This is not what BG wanted. Everything inside of him told him to let Gemo go and mob with somebody else. But Gemo was his blood and he really loved him. "Cuz, I got you. Just give me a few days."

Gemo smiled. "Aiight, cuz, bet that up!"

The two men sat talking about nothing for another ten minutes before Mane walked in. As usual the young hustler's swag was turned all the way up. A solid four karat diamond in each ear. BadLand fitted turned to the right. Crispy white *My Favorite Author* T-shirt over baggy blue True Religion jeans. And a fresh pair of white One's to complete his outfit. Slung over his right shoulder was a leather Nadia Terrell backpack.

"What's up, y'all boys?" Mane gave BG a slick right hand salute.

Raising his own right hand to his forehead, BG returned the salute. It was their thing. Whenever they saw each other they honored the union with a salute. BG was the general and Mane was his top lieutenant. "Just chillin', kid." BG looked at his G-Shock, then at Mane. "How you gon' spend all of that money on a gold Rolex and always be late?"

Sitting in the booth with BG and Gemo, Mane looked at the Rolex on his left wrist and shook his head. "BG, bruh, you wouldn't believe me if I told you."

"Yeah, well, it's probably something I don't wanna know," BG told his protégé.

Mane sighed and passed BG the designer backpack. "That's everything. And I'm out."

Unzipping the bag a little, BG peeped the stacks of dirty money. Gemo also peeked inside. And for a very brief instance, seeing the money made him hate Mane.

"Yo, let me get back to this bar…" Gemo got up. "Make sure you holla at me, cuz."

BG nodded.

"Aye, Gemo, let me get a Wet Wet." Mane tried to give Gemo two $20 bills.

Gemo looked at the money and then shot Mane an evil glance. *I'll get your lil' ass wet*, Gemo thought and walked away without saying a word.

"Damn, what's wrong with fool?!"

BG shook his head. "Kid's trippin'."

Before Mane could comment, a topless blonde waitress brought him a sixteen ounce cup of fresh frozen fruit – pineapples, strawberries, grapes, sliced apples, kiwifruit, and sliced peaches – with Bacardi Superior poured over it. Mane tipped the woman, then chewed a Bacardi soaked strawberry before asking BG, "So, when are you gonna holla at me?"

"I got you, lil' nigga. Don't I always make sure you're straight?"

Mane nodded and sipped his drink. "For sho'."

"And I always will… But, umm, did you take that car back?"

"Huh?"

"Lil' nigga, if you can *huh*, you can hear." BG frowned at Mane. "Now did you take that damn car back like I asked you to?"

"Nah."

BG shook his head sadly. "You wanna go to prison, huh?"

"Nah, big bruh."

"Yeah you do... You wanna go to prison and you wanna stay there for a long time. Because any nigga that's stupid enough to be sellin' dope and ridin' 'round in a $300,000 car, with no legal source of income, can't love his freedom." It seemed to BG that the more money Mane made the more he wanted to fuck up. "I told you that my man had a nice duplex in North Miami for $170,000 and you said you wanted it. Where's the money?"

"I'm gettin' it together now, big bruh."

"Gettin' it together? Mane, that was two months ago." Mane had been hustling good for three years with no major setbacks. "Mane, my nigga, how much do you have put up?"

"Like $80,000."

"What?!"

"A nigga livin', bruh. You know I ain't never had shit. Plus my ole-girl, my aunties and uncles. BG, I'm the man of the whole family. Whenever shit goes wrong, they come to Mane."

BG felt him, because shit had been the same way with him. But still, that was no excuse for only having $80,000 put up. Especially when you were moving as much dope as Mane was. *Plus this lil' nigga's givin' those people down at Prestige $3,500 a day for that damn Lamborghini*, BG mused. "Mane, with all due respect, that's bullshit. Because your people were makin' it before you made it in the game and they'll still be makin' it when you're doin' a hun'ed years behind this drug shit... I know they're family and you probably love them or whatever, but you can't let them misuse you, because I damn sure ain't gonna let you misuse me."

"Nah, big bruh, I wouldn't never try to use you." Mane's words were sincere. He really loved BG. And he would do anything for him.

"Mane, that's exactly what you've been doin'."

"How? Big Bruh, I always pay you yours on time."

"It ain't about that, kid."

Mane was confused and his facial expression showed it. "Then what is it about?"

"Do you know what assets and liabilities are?"

"Not like, exactly, but I know one's good and the other one is fucked up... You know, dealin' with money and shit."

BG nodded his agreement. "Assets are capital, resources, anything that's used to accumulate more money. Assets aid, they're advantages, my nigga... Now, liabilities are the opposite, they're debt, disadvantages."

"But how am I a disadvantage if I pay you on time, every time?"

"Because as soon as you pay me you go right back in debt, owin' me... A liability is owin', bruh, and anything's liable to happen in the streets. And whose gonna take that loss? Me, that's who! When I could've just sold the dope, straight up, and got my money on delivery, my nigga. I need you to have your own, Mane. That's when you become an asset to me, when I'm no longer takin' a risk and leavin' myself liable for your mistakes."

Mane just looked at BG. He knew then that he'd let his big homie down.

"You're bullshittin', Mane! Every minute I've spent talkin' to you, givin' you the game; every brick I've fronted you, traps I've bussed my gun to establish, were investments! I invested in you, kid. And lookin' at you now, my nigga, I invested bad. Because if I needed 200,000, funky-ass dollars, you couldn't give it to me! My niggas, my brutha, Fats, Stanka; France, my homies Bo-Jit, JackBoy and them, they died so that we could have this shit that we've got! That's why I respect this shit so much. That's why I guard this shit with my life! My nigga, that's why I can't stand back and watch you fuck it up. Because, my nigga, if we're not straight when it's all said and done, then they all died for *nothing*."

Mane was a tough little dude. At age 20 he'd seen and been through a lot. But as he sat there listening to BG, he was actually hurt, because he'd let his big homie down. All he could do was nod his head and take his chastisement. He understood, vowing to himself to do better.

"Mane, tell me something, and keep it one hun'ed... why do you hustle?"

"Shiid, because it's all I know. I mean, growin' up, when I was in school or out on the block, my friends, most of them, wanted to be football players or doctors and shit. But me, nah, I used to see niggas like you, Fats, LG and Lil One out there, pushin' whips and makin' moves. I seen the way that people respected y'all. And to me, that respect, the way that they treated y'all, that shit was greater than bein' the president of the United States, my nigga. So I knew ever since then that I wanted to be a gangsta, just like y'all. Because y'all did what y'all wanted to do, everybody else did what y'all let them."

BG felt that. He did not agree with it one hundred percent, but he respected it. Before he could finish schooling Mane, he heard a commotion coming from the front entrance.

"Angelina, just fuckin' can it, okay!? You're gettin' on my goddamn nerves, already. I should've left you home with your mother," Tony complained as he walked through the door.

"With all due respect, Dad, you can be such a jerk!" Angelina said, rolling her eyes.

"Yeah, that's just what she said."

"And who's *she*?!"

"Wouldn't you like to know?" Tony stopped and scanned the area. Spotting BG sitting in his usual booth, Tony smiled and walked over. "Well, if it isn't my favorite club owner."

BG laughed. "I'm probably the only club owner you know."

Tony slapped his own thigh and howled with laughter. "That could be it, BG!"

BG stood and hugged the big Italian police officer. They'd been friends for a little over two years. Ever since BG had moved his family out in Southwest Ranches, Florida, Devon had been playing football for PALZ league, which Tony oversaw. And being as BG spent a lot of time around Devon and his team – and also sponsored them every year by donating uniforms and signing a $80,000 check – he and Tony had become close. So close that Tony and his family were the only people that visited BG's house. The two families often ate at each other's house and exchanged gifts at Christmas.

"What's up there, Angelina?" BG greeted the unruly teenager.

"Hello, BG," she replied, showcasing pretty white teeth when she smiled. Her focused quickly shifted from BG to Mane. "Hello, Mane."

"Oh, what's up, Angelina?" He smiled brightly and got up. "I'ma go upstairs and play some games, let y'all two talk," Mane said to BG and Tony.

"Yeah, I'm goin' upstairs, too, Dad," Angelina chimed in.

"Go ahead, but no drinkin'! I catch you drinkin', I'll break your fuckin' lips. You understand," Tony threatened his 18-year-old daughter.

Angelina sucked her teeth and stomped off.

"You keep an eye on her, Mane. No drinkin'!"

"I got her, Tony." Mane walked off behind Angelina.

"Good, kid, that Mane. I really like that kid," Tony commented to no one in particular and sat down in front of BG.

BG pulled an envelope out of his pocket and slid it to Tony.

Tony accepted the envelope and peeked inside. Whistled. It was a check for $25,000 and $5,000 in cash. "God bless you, BG. I don't know what the kids at the center would do without you, pal."

"To whom much is given, much is expected. You feel me?" BG capped. "Now what do you have for me?"

Tony pocketed the envelope and began filling BG in on a few things.

Gemo wiped down the glass bar with a clean dry towel, watching the entire scene as it unfolded. He was always surprised to see that more women came into the topless bar than men on most days. The crowd was nice, though. And Gemo was happy that BG had finally decided to put him in the game. *Yeah, fuck all that ridin' the bench shit! I'ma starter,* Gemo thought to himself.

He saw that BG was still sitting with the big Italian with the big mouth. *Fake-ass, Louis Eppolito wanna-be,* Gemo thought, remembering the big *mafia cop* that he'd served a few years with in federal prison.

Gemo continued on down the bar, wiping, smiling occasionally at a nice looking honey, and saying hello to his regulars. Andras, the soft-spoken Hungarian, was still perched on his stool talking to his Spanish associate. Seeing that their glasses were empty, Gemo removed the used glasses and replaced them with two clean glasses, filled with ice. He then poured each man three fingers of *Black label*.

The two men never broke their conversation. "They are... ever seen any like them... only wants $1,200,000 for... valued at well over $3,000,000..." Gemo caught pieces of what the Spanish man said.

"I can only... because it will be difficult... bring me the diamonds... one week I... exactly $1,100,000... Nobody else will touch them." Gemo heard the Hungarian reply.

Diamonds?! Valued at over $3,000,000?! And these two suckas got them?! BG's interest was provoked. He dawdled a bit longer, slowly pushing his rag in small circles across the glass bar top.

"...man, Andras, you're killin' me... But what can... Have to make... My hands are tied."

"When can you… The diamonds as soon… The $1,100,000 will be in your hands… It's all on you."

"Tuesday comin'," the Spanish man replied.

Gemo noted that it was Friday. *Four days*, he thought and walked off.

BOOK 2WO

Death leaves a heartache that no one can heal... love leaves a memory that no one can steal...

—Anonymous

THE GIFT

Chapter 8

Nikkia got out of her car. She checked the address that she had written down and saw that it was the same as the address on the pale-green house. The house had a chain-link fence around it. Nikkia smoothed her formfitting black dress and took a deep breath before opening and entering the yard. She was so nervous. Her stomach was doing back flips. *The things we do for the niggas we love*, Nikkia thought. She wanted her man out of jail, but all of this was a bit much. Especially seeing as she did not *believe* as Haitian Jack believed.

Just as Nikkia made it to the porch, she heard footfall and heavy breathing behind her. She spun around and saw two big black Rottweilers running towards her. They were baring their large white teeth, preparing to tear hear apart. Scared shitless, Nikkia clutched her oversized purse and opened her mouth to scream. But nothing came out. She was literally petrified.

The dogs were about four yards from her, about to leap on her and most likely kill her right there in the front yard, but they suddenly stopped and just looked at her. Their eyes were red, scary looking. Yet there was something human in them. The Rottweilers were now looking beyond her. The man stood there quietly eyeing her. He was thin. Very thin. About six-foot-two-inches in height. His skin was as dark as the shiny black coats of the two Rottweilers. His eyes were a sick white, filmy and scary looking. Lots of tiny bumps covered his dark face and neck, like he'd been peppered with buckshots. He scared her worse than the dogs had.

"Come," he said. His Haitian accent was very pronounced. "I have been waiting for you."

"Me?!" Nikkia said, wondering how he could've been expecting her when no one besides her knew when she planned to come.

The house was dark, save for a few burning candles. Black blankets covered the windows. Absolutely no outside light shined into the house. Nikkia looked around. There was a large goat head on the wall. It looked as if it was looking at her. She quickly looked away. The house had a real eerie feeling. *What in the hell am I doin' here?!* she asked herself.

The scary looking black man took her hand, led her farther into the darkness. The candles flickered. A stifling scent assaulted her nose. Nikkia gagged and covered her nose with her free hand. It smelt like something or someone was in there dead. She was fully frightened now. *What am I doin'?!* she thought and froze. That was it. She could go no farther.

"Nikkia. It is okay. No harm to you," he said and pulled her along.

How the fuck does he know my name?! Nikkia wanted to know.

They stopped in a rear room. He sat her down on the carpeted floor. Left the room. Came back with a small cup. He sat down in front of her and handed her the cup. It was made of wood and was filled with a steamy liquid. It smelt like hot piss.

"Drink."

"Umm, what is this? And how do you know my name? Did you talk to Haitian Jack?" Nikkia asked nervously.

"Drink!"

Nikki hesitated. She really wanted to help her man. *Jack would never do anything to hurt me, so if he gave me this address then everything's gonna be alright,* she told herself and drunk the cup's content. "Aaaagh," she groaned, because the liquid tasted far worse than it smelt.

He took the cup and smelt it. He then placed the empty cup on the floor and took both of her hands into his. "I am Papa C. Me is bokor. Spirit prepare me for your visit," the man said and began chanting something in a foreign tongue.

Nikkia could feel her body heating up. *Dizzy.* She wanted to lay down. *Floating.* The man in front of her, Papa C, his eyes began to glow brightly. The room got hotter. His chanting got louder. A warm breeze swept over the room. And Nikkia could feel something that felt like hands caressing her all over, groping her breasts and rubbing between her legs. She gasped loudly, snatched her hands away from his, and everything stopped.

Papa C nodded his head. "Me no can do alone. Need help. Spirit say Papa Guede."

Nikkia was breathing hard. She took a minute to catch her breath. "Who is that? And how do you know that you can't do it if I haven't even told you what I want?"

"Boyfriend. You want out of jail. Spirit say Papa Guede."

This was unbelievable. He knew. "How, how much?" Nikkia asked.

"Not a lot of money for you boyfriend. $120,000 altogether. $70,000 now, $50,000 when Papa Guede come here from Haiti."

"From Haiti?"

"Papa Guede. Strong magic." Papa C stood. "Give me money now."

Nikkia stood up. She had exactly $70,000 on her. She gave him the money.

"Now, go see boyfriend. Him expect you. Tell him that me need..."

Nikkia listened carefully.

And when he was finished she left to go see Haitian Jack, just as he'd said.

Chapter 9

"Haitian Jack wants me to do what?!" BG shouted as he jumped up from his seat. He and Nikkia were in the living room of her Hollywood, Florida condominium. He'd arrived at her front door exactly one hour after concluding his meeting with Tony.

Nikkia looked at BG and shook her head. She already knew that he was going to hit the roof. Yet she had to ask because Haitian Jack really needed it done and he'd asked her to ask BG. "I know it sounds crazy, BG, but that's exactly what he said."

BG stopped pacing the carpeted floor and looked at Nikkia. The ex-stripper was dark as night and thick as a Wendy's frosty. Before Haitian Jack's arrest, Nikkia wore her thick black hair permed and flat-wrapped – it hung to the small of her back. But now she wore it short, like a man's. She vowed to keep it cut until Haitian Jack was once again free. But either way, with or without hair, Nikkia was a good looking woman. And best of all, she was loyal.

"You got something to drink in here?" BG asked her.

"Yeah. I have some wine coolers, Hennessey, Absolute, Bacardi Dark —"

"Bacardi Dark. Give me some of that," BG said. "I can't believe this crazy-ass shit."

When Nikkia came back from the kitchen, she handed BG a glass of ice and the bottle of brown liquor.

"Thanks, Nikkia." BG sat the glass down and took the bottle straight to the head. He swallowed deep and fought the burn of the strong liquor as it travelled down his throat and into his belly. Finally bringing the bottle down, BG hissed loudly and looked at Nikkia. "Now, tell me what exactly he said again."

Nikkia sighed with frustration and told BG everything from the beginning. And it seemed the more she explained it, the stranger and creepier the whole thing sounded. She'd never heard a request such as this and truly could not understand why someone would want such a thing done. Eerie. It was bizarre and mysterious. She thanked God that she was not BG, because as much as she loved Haitian Jack, there was no way on God's green Earth that she would have done it for Haitian Jack herself. Just the thought of doing something so sick and unholy gave her the heebie-jeebies.

When she was finished explaining it for the third time, BG turned the fifth of strong liquor up again and shook his head sadly. "Nikkia, you know this shit is crazy, right?!"

Nikkia nodded her head.

BG began pacing the floor again. "How soon?"

"Before trial... But, the sooner the better," Nikkia said softly. "They need time to work."

"This is crazy... This is so fuckin' crazy, yo." BG paced. The fifth of Bacardi Dark held tight in his hands. "Nikkia, do y'all know that this shit is illegal... Like, a nigga could really get fucked up doin' this shit."

Nikkia raised an eyebrow. *Nigga, everything you and Jack have been doin' since I met y'all has been illegal*, Nikkia thought but said nothing.

"I'ma do it." There was reluctance in his expression. "Just give me a few days... But let kid know that I got him, it's a go."

Nikkia did not know if she should have been happy or not. Things were just so strange. And she missed Haitian Jack so much. "I'll let him know."

"Yeah, you do that."

"And... Thank you, BG."

"Yeah... And thank you for the drink." BG placed the liquor bottle on the coffee table and walked out of the condo without saying another word.

Chapter 10

Through the five-foot stone and wrought-iron electric gate, BG parked his BMW in the big six car garage. A door in the garage brought BG into the house, through the kitchen. Monique, Devon, and his son LG were all seated at the kitchen table eating.

"BG, what's up?" Devon called out.

"BG, BG, BG!" LG said.

"What's up with y'all?"

"We're chillin'," Devon answered.

"Okay, you two, go and take a bath, get ready for bed."

Complaining, both boys got up and left the kitchen.

BG sat down in front of Monique. She could smell the liquor on his breath. She did not want to believe that it was another woman, because she loved him so much; and part of loving someone was trusting them.

"Are you hungry?" Monique asked.

"Nah, I'm good."

Monique looked at him with sad, worried eyes. Touched his hand. "Baby, what's wrong?"

BG shook his head. He didn't want to talk about it.

"Don't give me that, BG. You got up this morning, before first light, drinkin'. You've been gone all day, you haven't called, no texts, and here you come in after dark smellin' like a brewery! Something's wrong, baby, and I wanna know what it is because it's effectin' our family."

She was right and he knew it, but what good would it do to talk to her about it when there was nothing she could do to help him with it. Monique had never been in the streets. She'd never lost anyone to the violence of the streets. Demons did not haunt her dreams. There was nobody lurking the streets of Dade County waiting for her to slip so that they could rob and kill her. No, she did not understand. "I'm just goin' through somethin', baby, but I got a handle on it. Everything's gonna be aiight, ma." He forced a little smile.

"But, BG –"

"Monique, didn't you ask me to never bring the streets in our house?"

"Yes." She nodded.

"Okay. I've respected that. Now you've gotta do the same thing! I got this. Aiight?"

Monique slowly nodded her agreement. "I love you, BG, with all of my heart." A tear dropped from her right eye.

BG wiped it away. Kissed her. "And I love you more, Monique."

* * *

After a long hot shower, BG stepped from his bedroom's bathroom in only his boxer briefs. Monique lay beneath the cover, her back to him. BG eased into bed and saw that Monique was completely naked. Her brown skin smooth and flawless. The scent of her *Flora* by Gucci tickled his nose.

BG brushed Monique's long hair away from her neck and planted a kiss. Monique stirred and snuggled into him as he continued to kiss down her spine. He kissed each of her buttocks before spreading them and tickling her anus with his tongue. Monique moaned and pushed back into his thrusting tongue. Her spine tingled. Her fire had been ignited. She was now in that place where only BG could take her.

Monique, her face in the pillow, raised her ass and arched her back.

BG began stroking her clit with his tongue, provoking her womanly fluids.

"Oh, baby," she cried out, fingering her own erect nipples.

He left her clitoris and wedged his stiff dick inside of her.

Monique spasmed. Cried out. Bit the pillow and pulled at the sheets. He felt so good inside of her. As if God had fashioned BG's cock just for her – the gift. And she loved it.

BG gritted his teeth. Closed his eyes. His climax was at hand.

"Monique, baby, I loooove, you," BG groaned and released inside of her.

"I love you, too, baby," Monique answered, loving the feel of his warm fluids filling her. It was her gift.

* * *

The next morning BG was up early and out of the door. Instead of taking the BMW, BG decided to drive his 2014 Corvette Stingray Convertible. Money-green. Wide body. 460 horsepower. The $76,000 car was a gift from Monique.

BG stopped off at his El Portel residence and grabbed ten kilos of cocaine and quickly got back out in traffic. He'd slept good last night and felt refreshed. His mind calculating. A lot had been said between him and Gemo yesterday at the bar – more on Gemo's behalf than his own. He knew that there was some resentment in his big cousin's heart towards him. And maybe it was warranted. After all, Black Barbie had been murdered while scheming with him, so her blood was indeed on BG's hands.

Set a course, BG!

Maneuver along those lines!

You can never make everybody happy and stay true to yourself!

You have a design, stick to it!

BG did not know if these directives were coming from himself, the hustle-gods, or his beloved brother, LG, watching and guiding him from above. *All of this shit is so crazy*, BG thought as he cruised along.

Broke.

Motivated by poverty.

BG had only wanted something for himself and his people.

I didn't wanna kill ZoeMan... I know that ain't none of this shit worth my brutha and my dogs' lives...! Yet niggas act like I gotta gift... Nah, I'd give it all back to have my people back, because if I woke up tomorrow, with nothin' at all, as long as I got my heart I'll get it all again... BG thought.

Rick Ross' *I'm Only Human* poured through the slick Corvette's sound system.

BG turned right off of 103rd, on to 14th Avenue, and rode three short blocks before turning on to 101st Terrace. Three houses from the corner, on the right hand side of the street, sat a light-blue duplex. BG pulled in the duplex's yard and drove around to the back of the light-blue brick and stucco structure. There was a small single room efficiency behind the duplex. Brick and stucco. Light-blue as well. The white Lambo that Mane drove was parked beside the little house. BG frowned and got out.

This lil' nigga 'round here spendin' all this damn money on this hot-ass car, but got this lil' cheap-ass lay low, BG thought as he keyed the two dead bolt locks and entered the small dwelling. The living room, bedroom, and kitchen were all one room. There was a door that opened to a small closet and another door that led to the tiny bathroom. Mane was stretched out on the queen-sized bed, fast asleep. An open bottle of Ace of Spade sat on the nightstand, beside a baggie of colorful pills, about fourteen grams of purple haze, and a clipped blunt.

BG threw the gym bag, containing five of the kilos he'd just gotten from the stash-house, onto the bed with Mane. The bag landed on Mane's stomach, causing him to quickly sit up and reach for his gun. BG laughed and fired up Mane's half-smoked blunt. "It's a lil' too late for that, junior."

"Aiight, boy, bullshittin'," Mane said, his mind groggy. He'd been out partying all night. He popped two of the colorful pills and washed them down with the flat champagne.

BG shook his head. "Mane, you trippin'... why do you take those shits?"

"Shiid, big homie, you would take them too if you knew how they make a nigga feel."

Pills were not BG's twist. He'd only popped them once in his life. And that was the night he ended the beef with the Rich Kids. The only reason he'd taken the pills then was because his man Pimp had told him that liquor didn't affect you while on pills. And that night he needed to drink and appear drunk, but still have all of his faculties in order. Everything had gone as planned, however, the next morning he felt like he'd been drug through hell – tired, dehydrated, and running with diarrhea. *Nah, fuck that pill shit!* BG thought. "That's five right there, kid."

Mane grabbed the gym bag and got up out of the bed. "Aiight, give me 'bout four days, I got you, kid."

"Nah." BG shook his head. "Get me now."

"Huh?!" Mane was confused.

"Where's that $80,000 at?"

"Huh?!"

"If you can *huh* you can hear!" BG eyed Mane seriously. "Boy, get my money... Play time is over, kid-kid. You're 'bout to become a real asset or you're gonna get cut off with all of the other liabilities. You feel me?"

"Maaaaan," Mane said as he went in the closet. He fumbled around for a minute or two and came out with a Nike shoe box. "Here, man."

BG could see that Mane did not want to give the money up. "Now that you're spendin' your own money, you'll respect your profits more. And you'll thank me for the lesson later."

"Yeah, aiight," Mane sulked like a little kid.

"And you got two days to get me that $50,000."

"Maaaaan, I only owe you $45,000!"

"Nah, kid, it's a $5,000 tax for the front."

"Damn, BG!" Mane whined. "How I'ma do that in two days?!"

"Sell some ounces or *dirtbikes*. I don't give a fuck! Just have that cash, kid."

"BG, my nigga, damn..."

"Nah, Mane, it's tough love and you'll thank me for it later." BG saluted Mane and smiled.

Mane frowned, but he returned the salute.

With the $80,000 Nike box in hand, BG turned and left.

Chapter 11

"Angelina! Goddamn it, If you don't hurry your ass up I'm leavin' you! And you can fuckin' walk to the goddamn college for Christ sake!" Tony yelled from the living room.

"Tony Galletta, you don't have to curse at the girl like that!" Anne Galletta fussed.

"Gosh, Dad, I'm comin'!" Angelina yelled as she came down the steps carrying her designer book bag. Her pink blouse's top three buttons were unfastened, showcasing her firm 38-D's. Angelina loved her big breasts and flawless white skin, and she never missed an opportunity to show it. Her little skirt just barely covered her skinny thighs.

Tony looked at his daughter and sighed. "Where's the rest of your shirt and dress?!"

Angelina rolled her eyes towards the living room's high ceiling. Hot-pink lipstick covered her lips and her eyes were heavily shadowed with blue eye shadow. "Dad, I don't have time for this! If we don't leave now I'll be late, okay."

Anne mumbled something and took her daughter's arm. "Come on, dear."

Cursing, Tony followed them outside. He was stopped in his tracks at the sound of his daughter's loud scream.

"Aaaaaaaah! Oh my God!" she yelled, jumping up and down. She turned around and looked at her Dad. "Oh my God, Daddy, I love you!" Angelina then ran over and hugged him.

"I love you, too, honey."

Anne wiped at the tears building in her eyes.

Breaking their embrace, Angelina ran over to the shiny black Nissan 370Z. The car had a bright red ribbon on it and a custom front tag that read *Angelina G*. It was the best gift ever.

Tony and Anne walked over, arm in arm, as Angelina climbed inside and began adjusting the seat and mirrors. They were both smiling. Angelina was a good kid. She got good grades and never lied to her parents. So they did whatever they could to ensure her happiness.

"Make sure you wear your seatbelt, honey," Tony said.

"And no speeding, sweetheart," Anne chimed in.

"I will, Dad, and I won't, Mom." Angelina closed the door, started the engine, and kicked up dirt and gravel as she sped off.

Angelina could not believe it. She'd been begging her parents for a car ever since she turned 17, which was a year ago. Her dad would let her borrow his car on occasions, well, up until he'd bought the new Cadillac. Angelina was never permitted to drive that. But it didn't matter now, because she had her own wheels.

Should I go to school? she wondered. There were so many places she now wanted to go. Yet there was one person in particular that she wanted to see.

Angelina pressed her six-inch heel down on the 370Z's accelerator and smiled as the twin cams roared. She absolutely loved to go fast. Her dad had bought her the perfect car. It wasn't as fast as her boyfriend's car, but it was fast enough for her.

Awesome!

This is totally awesome, Angelina thought as she flew down the highway.

Chapter 12

Gemo stood behind the immaculate glass bar, drying glasses and overlooking the scene that played in front of him. *Boss players.* Suited and booted. Black and white. Some male, others female. Foreign and American. The people that walked through the doors of Wet Wetz everyday had chosen wisely in life, made the right sacrifices and put money in the proper places. They had *boss priorities* and very few morals. *Ethics?!* A substantial return on the principal was the only principle. And that's what made them bosses. Their ability to make the tough decision. Gemo felt that that was something his people, black people, lacked. Black people had too many morals, too much bible, and not enough common sense. *That's why we're so damn far behind in the business world,* Gemo reasoned. *But I'm 'bout to get mine... been a good nigga for too long!*

   He glanced down at his left wrist. The stainless steel TAGHeuer said that it was one-thirty. Placing the last of the dried glasses on the rack, Gemo discarded the used towel and pulled a fresh one from the bottom shelf. *Boss priorities foster boss character... Sacrifice the principle for the principal!* Gemo commanded himself as he wiped down the bar's surface. His eyes never strayed too far from the bar's entrance. Impassive. His dark-brown face betrayed no emotion. That is, until his buddy Andras Simonyi walked in. A sly grin appeared on Gemo's face as Andras took his normal seat at the far end of the long bar. His two Hungarian bodyguards posted up about three yards away from their boss.

Still smiling, Gemo placed a glass of ice in front of Andras and broke the seal on a fresh bottle of Black Label vodka. He poured the cool, mild mannered Hungarian three fingers of the expensive clear alcohol and sat the bottle down on the bar.

"Game seven, Eastern Conference Finals, what's the Heat gonna do?" Gemo asked, smiling.

Andras sipped his liquor and gritted his teeth. "Those damned Pacers are tough. But we'll spank them. And I'd sure like to be there to see that damn George's face when they go down."

"Yeah, I'd like to be there myself, but I gotta work." Gemo reached in his pocket and pulled out two slips of card stock. He had paid $70,000 for the tickets, which left him damn near broke. Gemo slid the tickets across the bar to Andras. "Three rows off of the court... Saved all year to get them..."

"You're kidding me, right?!"

Gemo shook his head. "I wish I was."

"Thanks, pal, what do I owe you? I know these things had to have cost you a fortune."

Again, Gemo shook his head. "Don't worry 'bout it. You just enjoy those tickets, from one Heat fanatic to another."

"I really don't know what to say."

"How 'bout, *go Heat!*"

Andras laughed. "Thanks, pal. I really appreciate this. It's probably the best gift ever."

Gemo patted the Hungarian on the shoulder and walked down to the other end of the bar. He saw his cousin coming in. Tossing the white towel aside, Gemo walked over and sat down in the booth with BG.

"What's up, cuz, what they do?" BG greeted him.

"They're doin' what they do, cuz. I'm just tryna keep them in order. You feel me?"

BG nodded. Waved a waitress over. The topless chick, one of only two African-American waitresses that worked in Wet Wetz, took BG's order and sauntered away.

"So what're we gonna do?" Gemo asked his younger cousin.

BG looked at Gemo real close before speaking. "I got you, cuz. This is not what I wanted, but I can't tell you what to do... Just know this, when I give you this, that's it. I don't sell weight and honestly, I love you too much to do business with you. So please, cuz, don't come back."

Gemo nodded his understanding. BG was cutting him off. "Aiight, cuz, I can live with that."

"After I eat, just follow me out to my car."

"Cool," Gemo replied and walked back to the bar.

BG could see that his big cousin was somewhat disappointed. But what else could he have done? He'd set a course and now he had to follow it. *You can't please everybody and be true to yourself,* BG reminded himself. Sadly, he shook his head. *And niggas think that I got a gift...*

Chapter 13

…They gon' remember me/ I said remember me/ so much money all your friends turn to enemies… And when it's beef I turn my enemies to memories/ where them bricks go for forty/ ain't no ten a key… (Hold up) Broke niggas turn rich/ love the game like Mitch/ and if I leave you think them pretty hoes gon' still suck my dick… It was something 'bout that Rollie/ when it first touched my wrist/ had me feelin' like that dope boy when he first touched that brick…

Meek Mill's *Dreams and Nightmares* boomed through Mane's little one room dwelling as he whipped up the work for the traps. Normally Mane dropped that *glass*, no whip. But after BG had talked to him and pointed out all of his flaws, Mane realized that he'd strayed from most of the things that Fats had taught him. His aim was to stack that money now. And whipping the work a little would add to his cash count. Especially since he now had to spend his own money.

At first, when BG took his $80,000, Mane was mad as hell with his big homie. But as he cooked the dope, reflected on what BG had said, then thought about all of the past conversations that he'd shared with Fats, he knew that BG was right. *I'm still gon' floss, believe that, but I'ma put some of this money up and invest in somethin' for my future… Because all of my dogs ain't die for nothin'! They gave their lives for my gift of life and I'ma make the best of it,* Mane thought to himself.

Mane had twenty ounces of crack cooked up when he heard someone banging on his door. He quickly turned the music down, put the crack cookies in the kitchen cabinet drawer, and walked over to the door. Only two people knew about his little *lay low* and one had a key, so this could only be the other.

Mane snatched the wood panel door open. The thick wrought-iron door still remained closed. "Bitch, what the fuck do you want?"

The young girl stared at him. "I want to see you."

"Stupid bitch, what the fuck I done told your ass about just poppin' up 'round here?" Mane had a mean mug on his normally handsome face.

"I know, but I'm your girlfriend," she said innocently.

"And what the fuck is that s'posed to mean, bitch?!"

She shrugged. "That I'm lucky... and special. And that I just missed you so much, I just had to see you, even if it meant you would curse me out."

Mane smiled.

She smiled back. Her smile was so beautiful. It was innocent and genuine.

Mane keyed the two dead bolt locks and let her in.

No sooner than the two doors were closed and locked she was in his arms, her large breasts pressed against him, their young tongues probing each other's mouths.

Mane loved the taste of her tongue, her smooth skin. He reached beneath her short skirt and squeezed what little ass she had. It was soft in his hands. Her breathing ragged in his ears. It was always this way when they came together.

The two of them had been doing this for the past year. It was something *different* for the both of them. Mane loved the fact that she was innocent and submissive. Her dedication to him sublime. For her it was his smooth, dark skin. His thug nature and the danger that it represented. In her young eyes, naïve and fanciful, Mane was a *bad boy* and she wanted nothing more than to be his *bad girl*.

Mane broke their embrace and took his clothes off.

She eyed his long black nature. It was the beginning and the end for her. She smiled. Her insides boiling. She could barely stand still, she was so hot with lust.

"Take that shit off!" Mane commanded her.

And she nearly tore the expensive articles of clothing trying to get them off. Once she was completely naked, she stood still, waiting for further instruction.

Mane just looked at her. His good little bitch. A year they'd been together. She was actually the closest thing he'd ever had to a real girlfriend. Every other chick in his life had just been a fuck. Because Mane always felt like they were trying to use him. So he used them first and discarded their asses like used condoms.

His hungry eyes took in the whole of her. Young. Taut. Even without a bra her juicy D-sized titties stood up. Her nipples long and pink. Enticing. Her long, silky black hair contrasted her skin, but complemented it perfectly. From her eyes, to her lips, to the way she walked and talked, everything about her was so sexy. The fact that she had a flat ass did not take anything away from her. In Mane's eyes it might've added to her physical beauty.

Mane kissed her again. Then spun her around. He squeezed her big titties as he stood behind her, his throbbing black dick pressed against her soft ass. She was so hot she felt as if she might flame up in his arms. Mane slipped his middle finger between her slick lower lips and teased her a bit. She moaned loudly. Mane quieted her by sticking that same middle finger in her mouth. She sucked it. She loved it.

"Ooooh, Mane, I'm so hot!"

He bent her over. Spread her legs and licked her soft-pink insides. Her juices were thick, sweet. Her moans were loud, pleading. She wanted his love inside of her.

"Baaabeeee, pleeeeeaaaase!" she begged.

With her hands on the bed and her legs gapped wide, Mane stood behind her and pushed himself inside. Her tight, wet cunt engulfed him. Slowly, he slid in and out of her. The muscles of her vagina working, trying to milk his dick of its cum. With each thrust he went deeper. Gasping, she bounced her pussy back to him.

Hot.

The small room had gotten hot.

A layer of sweat covered them both.

He could smell her sex as she released. It covered his black shaft. Encouraged him to pump faster and harder.

He could barely hear Meek Mill's *Maybach Curtains* playing as he fucked her.

"Maaaane, I love your cock... Please don't ever... stop giving it to me!"

"And, bitch, I love... your pussy!" Mane grabbed a handful of her long black hair and pulled it roughly. "So you... better not... give it to... nobody else!"

"Aaaaagh!" she screamed, climaxing again. "I looooove, yoooou!"

Mane pushed her all the way on the bed and turned her over. With both of her long skinny legs on his shoulders, Mane found her moist valley and quickly reinserted his dick. She yelled with each pounding stroke. Her pussy making loud sloshing sounds. Her big titties bounced to the rhythm of his thrusts.

Sweaty.

Frantic.

"Right there!" she cried. "That's my spot!"

Panting. Mane stroked her deep. "Daaamn," he moaned.

She knew that he was about to cum. And she wanted him to cum. But not inside of her. She did not want to get pregnant. But she also did not want him to stop. She closed her eyes and worked her pussy until she felt his warm spray shoot inside of her.

Mane released her legs and laid down on top of her. Both of them breathing hard, holding each other tightly. Satisfied. Mane was content. She was consumed.

Mane fired up a blunt. Hit it and passed it to her. While she was smoking he lifted the bag of pills and chewed two. Swallowed them dry.

"Mane," she whispered, passing him the blunt back.

"Yeah?"

"Can I have one?"

"One what?"

"One of those." She pointed at that baggie of pills.

"Hell nah."

She pouted. Laid there.

He hit the blunt and asked her, "You ever popped off before?"

"No."

Mane sighed and got the pill sack. There were some crumbs in the bag, maybe a quarter of a pill. He shook it out and gave it to her. "You start actin' stupid, I'ma put your ass out!"

She laughed. "I won't act stupid."

"Yeah, that's just what she said."

The girl looked at him. *My dad always says that!* she thought as she downed the crumbs. She felt nothing at first. But as they lay there, talking, laughing and holding one another, an intense wave of tension washed over her. She gritted her teeth and squeezed Mane to her tightly. Then the tension subsided. It was replaced with a feel she'd never felt before. In fact, it was the absolute best sensation she had ever experienced – better than orgasm. She looked into Mane's eyes and smiled.

"Aaaaw, shit," Mane said, knowing what was next.

She kissed him.

He pulled her on top of him and began massaging her ass as they swopped tongues.

Everywhere he touched her body ignited a new fire. Her body was vibing. "Ooooow, baby, I'm on fire!" she screamed.

Mane inserted himself and she began riding him.

Bouncing.

Bucking.

Cursing.

Orgasming back to back.

She was on a ride like she had never before experienced. And she loved it.

When Mane's nut finally came, she jumped up off of him and sucked his cum into her mouth, swallowing every drop of it. She had sucked dick before. But never had she swallowed cum. She was so open. She wanted to do everything with him. And they did. For the next three hours they had the time of their lives.

* * *

Three hours later, they were both sexed out, but full of energy. Mane knew that he'd fucked a whole day up. His phone had been ringing off of the hook. It was his workers calling for him to pick up their money and drop off more work, but he'd ignored their every call. So now the two of them sat at his foldout card table cutting and bagging up crack for the traps. Meek Mill's *Off The Corner* played as they worked.

Mane looked at her. She was mouthing the words of Meek Mill's song. When they'd first started messing around she didn't even know who Meek Mill was, now she knew his songs better than Mane. He smiled at her and said, "Lina, you're cool as hell to be a white girl."

"Okay, whatever," she replied and kept bagging up the drugs. She really liked helping him out. To her it meant that he trusted her. And to her trust and love went hand in hand. Over the past year she had probably bagged up more rocks than dudes that had been in the game all of their lives. Whenever she visited Mane they had sex and bagged up drugs. And most of the time he would leave, leaving her to do all of the work. But she did not mind – *trust and love*. And whenever he pissed her off, she did not argue with him, she simply cut the rocks too big. That always seemed to get him back in line.

Mane did not know what it was to love a female. Yet he did feel something special for her. He knew that money had nothing to do with what she felt for him. But what did? What was her motivation? he often wondered. "Lina, why do you fuck with me? Because I know that dudes with way more than I got be tryna holla at you."

She stopped bagging and looked at him. "Mane, now why would you ask me something so absurd, huh? You know that I love you because you look exactly like Young Turk from the Hot Boyz, *duuuuuh*," she said, laughing.

He laughed with her. "You got jokes, huh? But it's all good, because I know exactly why you be on me so hard."

"Because I love you."

"Nah. You love my doggy-style," he said and they both laughed.

The ringing of Mane's phone interrupted their laughter.

He looked and saw that it was BG. "Yeah?" he answered.

"I need you."

"When."

"Now."

"Okay."

"Aiight, I'm comin' through."

"Nah, nah, I'm walkin' out now. I can meet you."

"Cool. Write down this address."

Mane got the address and hung up. He looked at her. "I gotta go."

"Okay."

"You stayin' or leavin'?"

"What do you want me to do?"

"It's all on you."

"How long?"

"Maybe 'bout an hour or two."

She sighed. "Alright. I'll stay. But, please, don't be too long."

Mane kissed her and hit the door. But seeing the black car parked next to his Lambo, he stepped back in. "Who car?"

"Mine."

"Let me hold it."

She hesitated. "Okay." She tossed him the keys.

Mane caught them and was gone.

* * *

When Mane pulled up to the address, a house in Little Haiti, BG was leaning against a long black Suburban with dark tinted windows. One of Haitian Jack's men was standing beside him. Mane parked and jumped out.

BG saluted Mane. "Whose car?"

Mane returned the salute. "My homeboy's."

BG shrugged and got in the Suburban's driver seat.

Mane and Haitian Jack's soldier got in the backseat.

There were two other men already inside. One was Papa C, the tall Haitian with the pale eyes and keloid spots all over his face and neck. The other man sat in the Suburban's passenger seat. Medium build. He was almost white in complexion. His hair was long and thick, down his back. On his small head sat a sort of top hat. A black walking cane with a silver skull handle laid beside the mysterious man's leg.

BG put the big SUV in gear and pulled off.

Mane suddenly felt creepy. He looked behind him and saw that there were shovels, picks, and thick black tarps laying in the rear hatch. *Maaaaan, what the fuck is these niggas on?!* he wondered and felt for the gun on his waistband.

"You be okay," Papa C whispered to him.

BG brought the Suburban down 57ᵗʰ Street and 6ᵗʰ Avenue. He saw Gemo's dark-gray Range Rover parked behind King's forest-green BMW 750Li. The two men were standing in front of King's trap talking. *I wonder what Gemo's doin' fuckin' with king?* BG wondered. He also saw Mr. Fee sitting on his crate beside the store. He made a mental note to holla at the old man.

Taking a careful route, BG finally hit the on ramp to I-95, northbound. *I can't believe I'm doin' this shit,* he thought and drove on...

Chapter 14

There was a full moon out. The sky clear. A gentle breeze blew, low and constant, like the rustling of a money machine. Gemo stood beside his old friend, new business partner, and talked more business. A fat blunt passed between them. Their eyes low, but fixed on the line of fiends that ran back and forth to the *dozier* trap. Gemo had given the five kilos that he'd gotten from BG to King for an equal share of the dope spot. So far, from what he was seeing, it was a great investment. But Gemo was not finished making *tough decisions*. And being as he and King were already in bed together, he decided to bring him in on the real action.

"Yeah, everything's a go. $3,000,000 score, kid. But I've got a lot of time and personal resources tied up in this already, so I can only afford to hit you off with a $1,000,000," Gemo explained.

King nodded. Smiled. His gold-teeth shined in the dark. "Kid, that's love. I'm all in."

"Cool."

"What it is again?"

"Diamonds."

"Niggas or crackas?"

"Hungarians."

"Hungarians?!"

Gemo nodded. Looked around. He saw a dark Suburban pass. Wondered who was inside.

"When?"

"After game seven."

"What?!"

"Just be on standby, kid, cocked and ready to rock."

"Already," King answered.

The two stood quiet.

Cars passed.

The line of fiends never stopped or slowed.

Tough decisions... Too many morals... Gotta protect the principal, that's my sole principle... Everything else is pointless, Gemo thought to himself. He looked from the line of dope fiends to the man that stood beside him and then up into the clear night's sky. The moon was bright. Low. And briefly, for a fleeting moment, Gemo could have sworn he'd seen a face. The moon had frowned down on him. *Huh?* Gemo thought and rubbed his hand over his face. *I'm trippin'! It gotta be the 'dro fuckin' with me.*

"You good over there, kid?"

"Huh?" Gemo responded, snapping out of his thoughts.

"You aiight?"

Gemo nodded. "But I'll be better when we get this *cake*. You feel me?"

"Already, kid."

Dapping King up, Gemo jumped in his Range Rover and sped off.

Chapter 15

Mane cursed under his breath as he used the big bolt-cutter to snap a link in the heavy chain that secured the entrance gate of the cemetery. *Fuck am I doin' out here?* he asked himself as he swung the gates open. The black Suburban drove through. Mane closed the gates back and jumped in.

They drove around the large cemetery. It was dead quiet. The full moon was bright, shining eerily above them. Its light casting strange shadows in the dark. Mystified. BG circled the burial grounds until he found the section he was hunting. He stopped the big SUV and they all got out.

The fair-skinned import from Haiti, Papa Guede, looked around and nodded his head. He faced Papa C and rattled off a string of Creole.

Papa C turned to BG and translated. "Him say, rada loa is strong. But petro loa is stronger. And him say he is 99-years-old, his father is name Baron Samedi, who is the head of the Guede family."

BG looked at the fair-skinned Haitian man. He damn sure did not look 99-years-old. More like 40. His skin was milky white. His eyes dark. As black as the stone cross he wore around his neck. "What is rada loa or whatever you just said?" BG asked, wishing that he was somewhere else.

"Rada loa is good Voodoo loa's, spirits. Petro loa is bad Voodoo loa's, demons," Papa C explained.

This is a bunch of bullshit! That's what it is, BG thought. He did not believe in Voodoo.

Armed with an old machete, Papa Guede led them off through the many graves.

Papa C carried the old man's bag.

BG, Mane, and Haitian Jack's soldier carried the tarps, picks, and shovels.

This is so fuckin' bad, BG thought as they walked along.

They stopped in front of a tombstone marked, *Randolph 'Duke' Francis.* Papa Guede mumbled to Papa C in Creole. Papa C lowered the black bag to the ground and removed a small black pouch and a black cat. The poor animal's mouth and legs had been heavily taped.

BG shook his head sadly. *This is bad. Nothing good can come from this shit,* he told himself. He looked at Mane and saw that his little partner was just as confused and wary.

The old man, Papa Guede, removed his black cross and placed it on top of Duke's headstone. Duke was the man that Haitian Jack had shot to death for setting BG up to be busted by the Feds. Haitian Jack was now in jail, waiting to be tried for Duke's murder. Haitian Jack had always been heavy into Black Magic, the power of Voodoo. It was his belief. And in order to beat his case and once again be a free man, he needed Duke's spirit to work for him, being as Duke had been killed by his own doing.

Papa Guede said a long string of words in his native tongue. A brief appeal to his father, Baron Samedi, the lord of the demons and the dead. He then took the black pouch from Papa C and poured the gunpowder that it contained into three piles. Papa C then handed him the black cat. The bounded animal shivered in his hand. It was exactly one minute past twelve o'clock.

Mumbling and looking towards the full moon, Papa Guede sliced the cat's head off with the old machete. Blood spurted.

Flinging the animal's body about, Papa Guede splashed its blood over Duke's tombstone.

Mane turned his head to keep from vomiting.

The old man placed the dead cat, which had been a sacrifice to Baron Samedi, on the ground beside the three piles of gunpowder. He then knocked on the grave with the machete three times, calling Duke's names, asking the dead man to come forth and assist him in his work.

The three piles of gunpowder flamed up and the dead cat caught on fire. The flame was high. The smoke thick. The smell pungent.

BG jumped back. *What the fuck?!* he thought, wondering how in the hell had those piles of powder ignited.

Papa Guede, with blood dripping from his machete, raised his arms towards the dark sky and began chanting. A sudden breeze washed over them and whipped up and away.

Mane shivered. Looked towards BG. He was scared as hell.

Papa C walked over to BG. "The loa's have agreed… The spirit of the dead will help your friend, Haitian Jack. Now, dig up the body. Hurry!"

BG sighed and instructed his two men to help him.

Chapter 16

Mane sat at his little card table cutting up crack and bagging it for the traps. He'd been at it all day long. The spots were moving the drugs just as fast as he could get it to them. He knew that he needed to hire someone to help with the table work, but he really did not trust a lot of people. Besides, he'd been doing it so long, it was like therapy to him. He was actually relaxed when he was working the razor and bagging up rocks. It was his time to think. Often he reflected on the lessons that Fats had given him while they worked together at the table. He really missed Fats and wished that his deceased homie was there to see him now. To laugh with and help guide him through the drama that was his life.

Two days has passed since they'd excavated Duke's remains. Thinking about it still gave him the creeps. He'd never experienced anything so gross and weird. Twice the events from that night had followed him to sleep, haunting his dreams. That crazy night had also provoked a great deal of discord between him and his girlfriend. When he came in that morning, she'd been sitting at the card table crying.

"Where have you been, Mane?" she asked.

"Baby, I'm sorry, I swear."

"Where were you?"

Something told him to lie, but he felt that she deserved the truth. After all, he knew that she would've told him the truth. So

Mane sat down at the card table and held her hand. He looked her in the eyes and said, "Baby, this might sound crazy, but I was at a cemetery with BG and these Haitian dudes. One of them was white and couldn't speak no English. Lina, he worked a spell or some shit and called up the dead! Then he sacrificed a black cat and we had to dig up a dead body. That shit was cra—"

"Give me my keys!" she said and stood up. Her normally pretty face was a mask of anger.

"What?"

"Mane, you think that you can just tell me *anything* because I'm white?!"

"Nah." Mane stood up. "I swear!"

"I can't believe you! I put up with all of your shit! I know that you have other little friends, Mane, but I never bothered you about them because I figured if I was good to you and handled my responsibility as a woman, that you would realize what you had in me. It's been over a year! So I guess I was wrong." She was crying like crazy.

"Wrong about what? Lina, I'm not lyin'! I was really in a graveyard —"

"Save it, Mane. I'm white, but I'm not stupid!" She snatched her keys and walked out.

That was two days ago and Mane had yet to hear anything from her. He had called her cell phone a hundred times and left a hundred messages, but she would not answer or call him back. And that bothered Mane, because he did have feelings for her. But at the same time, he was not about to continue kissing her ass, because he hadn't done anything wrong. He'd told her the truth. *But hoes don't want the truth! They wanna be lied to. But she'll be aiight*, Mane convinced himself. Yet inside, he really did miss her.

* * *

Mane made his rounds, riding all over Dade County dropping off work and picking up money. His cell phone rang constantly. And each time he was disappointed to see that it was not his girlfriend. He wanted to talk to her so bad. *Crazy-ass white bitch,* Mane thought and continued on his money route.

After making his last two drops, Mane parked the clean blue Bubble Caprice in his mother's backyard, ran in the house to put up some money, and came back out, passing the Caprice up for the extravagant Lambo. He jumped in and peeled out. Meek Mill's *Young Kings* played as he rode.

He made two more stops.

The pill man – he bought one hundred pills.

The 'dro man – he bought an ounce of Cush.

Now, literally *rolling* and smoking as he rode, Mane just roamed the streets aimlessly. Ever so often he'd see Duke's skeletal remains in his mind. The rotted flesh, just barely clinging to the bone in some areas – most of it having already been eaten away by maggots. It might have been a million of them eating at the dead man's flesh. And the smell?! What Mane had seen that night was the true definition of hell.

When I go, gotdamn it, I'm gettin' cremated! Mane concluded. *Fuck all that maggots eatin' a nigga and crazy Haitians diggin' a nigga up tryna make a nigga work for them and shit... Shit done fucked up my relationship and all.*

Ten minutes later he was parking at his *lay low.* He had made up his mind. He was going to get fresh, hit a few clubs, and have him some fun. He needed to forget about Duke's dead-ass and his torn relationship.

Chapter 17

BG pulled up to the two-story white and black house that he'd leased for Papa Guede's stay in Miami. The house was on 15th Street and 14th Avenue, just a stone's throw from the county jail. The Haitian bokor had insisted that the house be within a mile of the courthouse, the closer the proximity the greater his ability to work his magic. The location was perfect.

BG got out of the car carrying the items that Papa Guede had asked for: The suit that Haitian Jack planned to wear to court, Haitian Jack's $65,000 Rolex, and the $50,000 balance on the $120,000 that they were being charged for the bokors' service.

When BG got to the door it swung open. Papa C stood before him. His dark, spotted face stoic. He stepped aside and gestured for BG to come in. A wall of funk hit BG as soon as he stepped in. There were small cages with cats, dogs, and chickens scattered throughout the living room. All of the poor animals stood quiet, as if they actually felt the evil and knew that they were certainly going to die. BG felt bad for them. *Damn, this shit is so fuckin' bad!* he thought, shaking his head sadly.

Papa Guede sat in an eastern corner of the room. He mumbled something in Creole.

"Him say, come to him," Papa C explained.

BG walked over and gave the man Haitian Jack's suit, Rolex, and the money. Their hands touched briefly.

The fair-skinned old man turned to Papa C and spoke to him in Creole. Papa C left the room and came back with a wooden cup and a small palm tree. He gave them to the old man and stepped back.

Papa Guede drunk from the cup and spat a spray of the liquid on the palm tree. He spat another spray on Haitian Jack's Rolex. Then, placing the Rolex in a small black pouch, he shook some of the dirt from the palm tree's root into the pouch and tied it close. With palm tree in one hand and the pouch in the other, Papa Guede began chanting loudly. When he was done he spoke to Papa C.

"Him say to plant tree in your backyard, very close to house, under your window if possible. Then, take watch and throw in ocean. Check tree every day. You know if friend come home," the tall Haitian man explained.

Throw a damn $65,000 watch in the ocean, huh? These two niggas are crazy! BG reasoned as he took the palm tree and the pouch from Papa Guede. He turned to leave. But before he could exit the house, he heard the old man's distinctive chatter.

"BG," Papa C called out. "Him say you are in danger."

"What?!" BG looked at the two men.

Papa Guede spoke again to Papa C.

"Dangerous white man. Burn. Him say protect your chest from the woman. The fire."

BG frowned his face. "What the fuck is he talkin' 'bout? What woman?! What does he mean, protect my chest?"

The old man said a few more words. Nodded his head and waved his hand.

"Him said old friend mean you no good. Cause woman to throw fire. Protect your chest. Or you die." Papa C walked over and opened the door for BG.

BG sighed loudly and exited the house.

Confused.

A bit wary.

BG drove straight home and planted the palm tree a foot off of the house's foundation, below his bedroom window. He then drove off to the pier on Key Biscayne, and against his better judgment, he threw the black sack containing his best friend's Rolex into the roaring ocean. *There goes $65,000,* he mused and drove off.

Beanie Sigel's *Feel It In The Air* played as he rode.

He sparked a pre-rolled blunt of purple and thought. Everything was so surprisingly peculiar. He thought about last night, Duke's decaying corpse, and the things that the two bokors had just told him: *You are in danger... Dangerous white man. Burn. Protect your chest from the woman. The fire... Old friend mean you no good. Cause woman to throw fire. Protect your chest. Or you die,* Papa C had translated. But BG did not believe in soothsaying or black magic. So why was he worried? Why did he feel the need *to protect his chest?*

BG jumped on the expressway and headed home.

Chapter 18

Kadar got up from the weight bench. A thin layer of sweat coated his six-foot-four-inch, 250 pound body. The big Hungarian was shirtless. His huge pectoral muscles and twenty-inch biceps were swollen from his intense workout.

Kadar drunk from his bottle of vitamin water and then slid three more forty-five plates on each side of the weight bar, bringing the total weight to 495 pounds. Kadar laid back down on the big Olympic bench, inhaled deeply, and lifted the weight. He brought it down slowly and rocketed it back up quickly. He repeated that twelve times before racking the weight.

He got up to place four more forty-five plates on the bar, but stopped at the ringing of his cell phone. The ID told him that it was Ferenc, the nervous little *consulere* of his boss and mentor, Andras Simonyi. "Hello?"

"Kadar."

"Yes, what is it?"

"You are needed. Come to the house now."

The house could only be one house, Andras Simonyi's house, because he was *the boss*. "Okay, I'm leaving now." He hung up and exited his big home gym. Thinking. There had been urgency in Ferenc's request.

"You finished already?" Koka, Kadar's sexy and overly aggressive sister, asked as he came through the living room toweling off his upper body.

"Get ready to go," he said and kept on walking to his master bedroom.

Koka, at six-foot tall, was the exact female version of her brother. She stood up from the couch and headed to her own room.

* * *

The sleek snow-white Audi A8 came to a stop in the circular driveway of Andras' two-story house. Koka exited the driver's side. Kadar got out on the passenger side. They were met at the door by Ferenc. The greeting was short. He quickly walked them to the living room, where one of Andras' bodyguards and Andras' wife, April, both lay dead. They'd both been shot through the back of the head. Their blood covered the couch and carpet.

"What is this?!" Kadar asked, his facial expression a mixture of anger and sadness.

Ferenc said nothing. He gestured for them to follow him and walked off.

At the top of the stairway they stepped over the other dead bodyguard.

Kadar's blood boiled. A knot formed in his stomach. He already knew whose dead body he was going to see next.

When they entered Andras' master bedroom they found the Hungarian mafia don facedown on his oversized bed. The back of his head had been blown completely off. Blood had soaked through the mattress and leaked onto the carpeted floor. Kadar turned and walked out of the bedroom. Had he not been such a strong man he would've surely broke down and cried. Andras had been more than a boss to him. The man had been a friend and a father figure to him.

Ferenc and Koka came out into the hallway and stood before him.

"What happened?" Kadar asked, his voice a shallow whisper.

"I called him all morning. No answer. I found that strange because we were supposed to meet this morning. So I came over. Opened the door and found this mess. I called you," the nervous little man explained.

"Why were you two meeting?"

"Diamonds. Three point six million dollars. I had them sold for him."

"Anybody else know about the diamonds?"

"No. Not on my end. Maybe April knew."

Koka just listened and looked on.

Kadar sighed and walked off. Back inside of Andras' room, Kadar sat down at his boss' red oak desk. Turning on the computer, he pecked at the keyboard and smiled. "Amateurs," he said, pleased to see that the home security cameras were still activated and the recorded data on its board was still intact. "Call someone and get this place cleaned up before you call the authorities," Kadar ordered as he disconnected the computer's tower and left with his sister.

Chapter 19

BG got dressed and was prepared to leave the house. It was still dark outside. He'd had another nightmare. Only in this one he was being hunted by a group of white people. *Police?* He was unsure. However, he remembered the Haitian man's words: *You are in danger... Dangerous white man. Burn. Protect your chest from the woman. The fire... Old friend mean you no good. Cause woman to throw fire. Protect your chest. Or you die...* BG thought. He was confused about the old man's words. What did they mean? BG rubbed his hand over the chest area of his shirt. *I'm protected*, he told himself and headed for the door.

"BG!" Monique called.

He turned to face her. She stood there in her housecoat, watching him. Her expression was a mixture of fear and disappointment. "Baby, what's wrong?" BG asked her.

Monique covered her face with her hands and started crying.

BG quickly walked over to her. Held her to him. "What's wrong, Monique? Why are you cryin'?"

"I'm tired, BG... I'm tired of you leavin' me every morning before sunrise! Is she that much better than me?" She was crying uncontrollably.

"Who is *she?!*"

"Why don't you tell me!"

BG hugged Monique tight and kissed her forehead. "Monique, it ain't no she."

"Then why are you so distant?" She looked up into his eyes. "Why do you always wake up and leave me every morning?"

"Because I have to! Monique, I have a job that comes with a lot of pressure."

She said nothing. She just stared at him. Her expression said that she wanted to believe him, but that she needed a little more in the way of an explanation.

"Monique, baby, do you love me?"

"Un... con... ditionally," she said between sobs.

"Then you gotta trust me... I'm in this for us! I bleed those streets for the benefit of our family. I sit in that bar and politick all night so that Devon and LG won't have to go through the shit that me, my brutha, and all my homeboys had to go through... Baby, I barely get to see you and spend time with the kids, so how I'ma have time for some bitch?"

Monique stared at him. Slowly nodded her head.

"Come on," BG said, taking her by the hand. He led her through the kitchen and into the garage.

"BG, baby —"

"Nah, bring your ass on! You wanna see where I'm goin' and why I can't sleep, I'ma show you." He pushed her into the passenger seat and walked around to the driver's side.

"The kids, BG —"

"They'll be aiight 'til we get back." He cranked the car up and exited the garage.

The drive to the stash-house on 118th Street was quiet.

He parked the car and pulled her inside the house. They went straight upstairs to the master bedroom. BG pulled a box open and dumped the money out.

Monique looked and covered her mouth.

BG opened another box and dumped it out.

She couldn't believe her eyes. She knew that BG hustled and had money, because they lived a good life on top of what she brought to the table, but she did not know that he was getting money like this. Monique figured that the money she had helped him *wash* through her beauty salons, the money that he'd used to open up the bar, was all of his illegal money.

"Every box in here is fulla money. Money that my brutha and my homeboys died for! Close to $8,000,000. And I can't sleep knowin' it's just sitting here in this room. I gotta 'nother house with another $7,000,000 worth of cocaine in it... I can't let nothing happen to it. I've lost too much over this shit already... Every night I have nightmares of somebody stealin' my shit or tryna kill me over it... That's why I can't sleep. Can't enjoy my life. Can't do shit 'til the drugs are gone and the money's safe, otherwise, my people died for nothing..."

Monique hugged him. Kissed his forehead, his eyelids, his nose, and then his lips. She understood. And she felt foolish about her insecurities. "I'm sorry, BG... I'm so sorry, baby."

BG kissed her lips while removing her housecoat. In no time at all they were both naked, on the carpeted floor expressing their love for one another.

"I... love... you... BG!" Monique exclaimed.

"I love you, too, baby... And I want you to be... to be my wife," BG whispered in her ear as he fucked her nice and slow. "Monique, will you... marry me?"

She was so overwhelmed with joy that she couldn't speak. Tears streamed down her pretty dark-brown face as she nodded her head *yes*.

BG smiled. Kissed her with all of the passion that he had inside of him.

Their bodies came together with force. Slapping and gripping. Passion's conflict. Love's collision. With half a million dollars scattered on the carpet beneath them, they made love until the sun came up.

"...always look several steps ahead and plan accordingly... [But know that] playing on people's weakness has one significant danger: You may stir up an action you cannot control."

—Robert Greene

THE CURSE

Chapter 20

Judge Anderson was a mean, grumpy old man. Round and bald. Pale with beady pig eyes. He'd been ruling over the criminal courts in Dade County for the last forty years, which was ten years longer than any eighty-two year old man should've been residing over the courts. But Judge Anderson had vowed to hand out a million year in prison sentences before he retired and he aimed to do just that. Besides, Judge Anderson hated change just as much as he hated criminals and senseless formalities.

Exiting his big ranch-style home, the judge placed his large bundle of clothes on the passenger seat and climbed into his new model Lincoln and pulled off. A new rendition of Beethoven's *Sixteenth Symphony* played as he rode along.

Humming and tapping his hand against the steering wheel, he thought-out his day. He had to first drop his laundry off at the cleaners, get a fast bite to eat, then begin studying the elements of the murder trial that had fallen to him. *Work, work, work,* Judge Anderson thought. But then again, he loved his job. He felt his purpose in life was to scourge the heathens of the earth.

Having finally arrived at the cleaners where he'd been getting his clothes done for the last twenty years, the good judge grabbed his laundry and climbed out of the car. The sun was deadly hot. It seemed that God had turned the temperature up a bit since he'd left home. Judge Anderson wiped at the sweat that had settled on his wrinkled brow and lumbered off to the building's entrance. The bell on the door rang as he walked in. A terrible smell assaulted his long, hooked nose. He frowned and looked to the long counter, expecting to see Henry, the owner of the cleaners. But Henry was not there. No, a tall black man with bumps covering his face and neck stood behind the counter. He had the scariest set of eyes the judge had ever peered into.

"Where is Henry?" Judge Anderson asked, covering his nose with his free hand. The place smelled like raw sewage.

"Him is in the bathroom. Very sick," the man explained. "Something him ate, I'm sure."

The judge shook his baldhead and thrusted the bundle of laundry at the man. He was about to say something further but quickly decided against it. He just wanted to get out of the stinking building, so he turned and left.

As soon as he saw the judge's Lincoln exit the parking lot, Papa C picked up the bundle of clothes belonging to the grumpy old judge and exited the cleaners also. His mission had been accomplished. He smiled as he got into his old Honda Accord and sped off. *One step closer to getting Haitian Jack back in our good graces,* he thought. Everything else was already in place. The personal effects of the presiding judge was the last thing they needed and now they had it… Yes, it seemed that Baron Samedi and the loa's were indeed on their side…

Chapter 21

BG stood behind the long glass bar fixing drinks and greeting customers. It was a quarter past twelve o'clock and he'd been at it since ten. Friday night was ladies' night at Wet Wetz, which made it one of their busiest nights. Not only did the ladies get in free before twelve o'clock, but their drinks were half-priced and there was a fully nude male review. So Friday nights were always packed to capacity.

As BG filled drink after drink, he scanned the crowd and watched the entrance as often as he could, hoping that Gemo would come in. He'd been calling his big cousin for three days now, no answer, only the voice-mail. BG had left him several messages, but Gemo had yet to respond. He also had not been back to the bar since BG had given him the five kilos. *I hope cuz is* alright, BG thought, questioning his own decision to give Gemo the five *bricks*.

The DJ spun Chris Brown's *Loyal* just as BG spotted Mane walking towards the bar. The young hustler was sporting an 8732 jean set, a tight white-T, crispy white Air Force One's, and about $250,000 worth of chains, rings, and bracelets. A big Gucci backpack was slung over his shoulder. A light skin dude of medium build seemed to be trailing Mane. The dude wore a black Dickie, black One's, and a red Hustle Gang hoodie.

"What's up, Big Gangsta?!" Mane greeted BG, giving him a crisp salute.

BG returned the salute. "I'm good... Yo, who is kid, he with you?"

Mane looked at his little man. He had trailed off and took a seat at a near table, watching Mane and peeping out the scene. Mane smiled. "Yeah, that's Sadam. He's my shooter."

BG nodded, looked at the young dude. He was probably about sixteen-years-old. "Yo," he said, turning back to Mane. "You havin' some kind of problems? Niggas actin' up?"

"Niggas can act up if they want to, but I promise, when I squeeze it hurts!"

"We'll lose two lives, yours and mine."

"Give me any amount of time, just don't let my ROC niggas grieve."

"In the funeral home cryin', drippin' tears on my sleeves," BG finished the motto that they often recited together. The words were from Jay-Z's *Lucky Me*. He smiled as he took the backpack from Mane and placed it under the bar. It was money for seven kilos. Mane had become an asset. "If you're good, why are you ridin' with a shooter?"

Mane shrugged. "Just spendin' some time with kid. I got love for him, but at the same time, bruh, I've been feelin' creepy ever since we dug that body up."

BG rubbed his hand over the material covering his chest. "I feel you... I've been feelin' crazy myself." BG cracked the seal on a fresh bottle of Bacardi Dark and poured three fingers in two glasses. One he slid to Mane, the other he sent over to Mane's shooter, Sadam.

Mane sipped his drink. "So, umm, BG, what do you think 'bout all that crazy-ass Voodoo shit?"

BG shrugged. "I don't, kid, I don't think about it at all. That's Haitian Jack's belief, his way of life. I really love him, so I did what I needed to do for him, regardless as to how I felt about the shit, just as I hope you and him would do for me if it came down to it."

"Maaaaaan, big homie, you already know. It's ROC to the death of me. I ride and I ride for you, bruh," Mane proclaimed.

"Nah, lil' nigga, don't ride for me, ride for the cause. Ride for what's right, what's seated deep in your heart. Because if it's me you're ridin' for, who will you ride for when I'm gone?"

Mane sipped his liquor. Thought. BG was right. "I hear you, bruh."

"Nah, kid, fuck that *hear* me shit. Do you *feel* me?"

Nodding, Mane said, "Yeah, bruh, I feel you."

"Aiight then. But let me get back to work, these damn drinks ain't gonna serve themselves."

Mane saluted BG and sat down at the table with Sadam. Then, removing his pill sack from his pocket, he passed Sadam one and popped two himself. The two of them had been popping pills and moving around selling drugs all day. Mane still hadn't heard anything from his girlfriend, but that was cool. He missed her, but he was finished with stressing over the situation.

The two sat there, drinking and rolling, watching the miscellany of beautiful women dancing and enjoying themselves. As they sat, vibing, Mane noticed a pretty red-bone eyeing him. She had blonde hair and nice C-cups. The short formfitting dress accented her hips and showcased her shapely red thighs. She was a dime.

They held each other's stare. She smiled, seductively and knowingly. Mane smiled back as she walked over.

"What's up, Mane?" she asked and took a seat beside him.

"Ain't shit, Mariah, what're you doin' in here?"

"Shiid, vibin' and lookin' for you." She picked up Mane's drink and sipped from his glass.

"Why're you lookin' for me?"

"So we can talk. You said that we could talk some more when I got something, well, here," she said and handed Mane a stack of crispy *big face hundreds.*

Mane looked at the money. He couldn't believe that Mariah had given it to him. In his book she was a class-A gold-digger.

"So you don't remember?" she asked.

"Yeah, yeah, I remember. I just can't believe you're givin' me this money."

"Well, don't, because I'm not. I'm investin' that money in us, because I need you to know that I dig you on another level. You feel me? I thought about the shit you said that day after you fucked me and dismissed me like I was yesterday's fade... I'm not gon' front, though, or try to be hard, that shit hurt my muthafuckin' feelings. But at the same time, I respected it because you had a right to feel that way, and what you said was real. A nigga shouldn't want no female that ain't got shit and ain't tryna do shit for herself. So, hey, I'm grindin' and I'm tryna fuck with you."

Damn!? Mane thought. "Who're you here with?"

"Two of my homegirls."

"Well, I'm in the Lambo, so they gotta take my man home."

"That ain't no pressure."

"Well make it happen and we're outta here."

She got up, her big ass swaying as she walked over to her homegirls to let them know what was up.

Mane smiled. He had never heard anything so real come out of a female's mouth before. Pocketing the money that she had given him, he saluted his man Sadam and left Wet Wetz with Mariah.

Chapter 22

Two o'clock was flashing on the big neon clock. BG watched Mane leave the club with a bad red-bone. *This lil' nigga 'bout to go and get it in and I'm stuck here servin' drinks*, BG thought. He was tired and ready to go home to his lovely fiancée Monique. Just two days ago, after he had made passionate love to her and proposed on the money littered floor of his stash-house, BG had made things official by buying Monique a $150,000 engagement ring. They were set to get married in thirty-six days. He truly loved her and vowed to protect her and love her forever.

BG had just fixed two Wet Wetz for a gay female couple when Gemo and King walked in. The two were dressed to the nine's and turning all heads. Gemo wore dark-blue, loose-fitting jeans, a two-button black suede cocktail jacket, black and blue plaid button-down shirt, and black suede slip-in shoes. The whole outfit was Gucci and costed Gemo a pretty $4,390. And that did not include the black diamond chain that he wore.

King wore a two-piece *Dame Dash Signature* suit. White in color. Matching Gucci slip-ins. Two strings of big clear diamonds hung from his skinny neck. The two men looked exactly how money was supposed to look — *damn good*.

"What's up, lil' cuz?" Gemo greeted BG as he took a seat at the bar.

King sat down beside him. Nodded at BG. King knew BG, had known him for many years, but they never really clicked as far as friendship.

BG returned the nod and directed his focus at his cousin. "Damn, kid, what's good? We beefin' or somethin'? Because I've been callin' you for three days now. What's up with that?"

Gemo smoothed the material on his coat sleeve before saying, "Nah, cuz, I've been busy as hell, *gettin' it how I live,* you feel me?!"

"I see that. You're lookin' like money."

"Yeah, me and King just flew in on something private, you dig? Been up in Atlanta negotiatin' a few things with some big boys I met in prison. But I figured that I'd at least holla at you one more time before I locked in with them, because you might want this money we're tryna spend," Gemo explained.

"What're you talkin' 'bout, cuz?"

"I'm talkin' 'bout $2,000,000."

BG frowned. "Y'all two tryna spend two tickets?"

"Yeah."

"Y'all money?!"

"Yeah, nigga! Who else money would we be spendin'?"

Where the fuck did these two niggas get $2,000,000 from?! BG wondered. "That's a lot of *cake,* bruh," BG said, shaking his head.

"Yeah. And we're tryna spend it. My peoples in Atlanta talkin' 'bout $19,500 a bird. What's up?"

BG shook his head again. $2,000,000 was a nice *lick.* But he had already set his course. So to change directions now would be contrary to his better judgment. "Nah, cuz, you better jump on that $19,500, because I ain't in no shape."

Gemo shrugged. "Aiight, cool, but give me a bottle of that *Black Label* vodka." He placed $500 on the glass counter. "I wanna drink to an old friend and my newfound fortune."

King bussed out laughing and slapped five with Gemo.

BG did not bother to inquire. He simply picked up the money and got them their bottle and glasses.

An old number by the O'Jays, *Back Stabbers*, came on. BG knew the song. His aunt had often played it when he was young. But he'd never heard it being played in his club. *Strange*, he thought as he worked his way down to the other end of the bar. BG piled a bunch of glasses into the dishwasher and started the machine. When he looked up again he got another strange surprise. Coming through the club's entrance at two-thirty was Tony Galletta. The big Italian lawman spotted BG and quickly made his way over.

"Give me a fuckin' drink, will ya." Tony sat down at the glass bar. He looked tired and frustrated.

"Well hello to you, too, big guy," BG said, pouring his friend a double-shot of Bourbon on the rocks.

Tony gulped the drink down in one big swallow and pushed the glass towards BG, who filled the glass and slid it back. "Hey, don't go gettin' sensitive on me, for cryin' out loud. I thought BG stood for Big Gangsta."

BG just shook his head and laughed at the wise guy wannabe. Tony was funny, but he was a good dude. "Tony, man, what the hell are you doin' in here at damn near three o'clock?"

Tony sipped his drink. Chew a piece of ice. "Down at the fuckin' precinct. Place is a goddamn madhouse. Big, big case… The don of the Hungarian mafia got clipped. Some idiot killed Andras Simonyi, his wife April, and you should see this skirt, she was a real looker." Tony whistled and shook his big head. "They also killed two of Andras' goons. Execution style. *Bang!* Right in the back of the melon."

"Any suspects?"

"Not a fuckin' clue. And to make matters worse, Angelina's about to give her poor mother a fuckin' heart attack! For Christ sakes, ever since she got that goddamn car it's been one fuckin' episode after a fuckin' 'nother. Stayin' out, gettin' up late, missin' school, the goddamn girl's lost her fuckin' mind and she's tryin' her damnedest to drive me and her mom into the nut farm with her."

BG poured his friend another drink. "It'll be aiight, champ. Angelina's a real smart girl. She'll snap back."

"Yeah, I sure hope so, because I'm fuckin' gettin' sick of it! I gotta go home now, after fourteen hours at the goddamn station, and listen to Anne bitch about Angelina, that goddamn car, and what Angelina's doin' or ain't doin'. I fuckin' swear to you, BG, another week of this, and I'm gonna go fuckin postal." He stood up from his stool and sat a ball of crumbled up bills on the bar.

"Well, don't come in here with that frustrated white man shit and shoot nobody in here," BG told him, lifting the money from the bar.

"Speakin' of comin' in here, BG, has Angelina been in here?" Tony asked.

BG shook his head. "Nah, not in 'bout four or five days."

Tony sighed. "Well, BG, pal, if you happen to see her before I kill her... would you, you know, have a little talk with her, will ya? She seems to value your word, you know."

"Not a problem, Tony. Angelina's like family to me, so anything I can do to help right her ship, bruh, consider it done."

"Thanks, BG," Tony said and left.

BG nodded and continued down the bar, wiping in small circles with his towel. It was five minutes till three o'clock and the crowd showed no sign of thinning.

"Cuz," Gemo called from down the bar. He was feeling good. It seemed his ship had came in and his luck had changed. BG walked down to where Gemo and King sat with two sexy white chicks hugged up beside them. "You sure you're not tryna get this money? We're fam, cuz, and when it's all said and done, we're really all we've got. You feel me?"

BG wanted to do it, to help his cousin get right, because it was obvious that Gemo was serious about his *cake*. $2,000,000 was a lot of money to be shopping with. Yet something inside of BG warned him against taking that money. Maybe it was the fact that King had something to do with the situation that made BG leery. Whatever the case, he could not do it. "I wish I could, cuz, but I'm not in position."

"Aiight," Gemo said and shrugged.

Looking at the flashing neon clock, BG saw that he had one more hour. He sighed and continued down the bar, wiping and wishing he was at home with Monique.

Chapter 23

BG walked slowly to his car. The backpack of money that Mane had given him earlier was slung across his shoulder. He was so tired and ready to crawl in bed. *I gotta hire somebody to run the bar since Gemo's not comin' back*, he told himself as he walked.

A few of the club's patrons and employees were scattered about the parking lot, either going to their cars or trying to *couple up* for the night. One woman in particular caught BG's eye. She was tall. Her lithe body was wrapped in a tight red silk dress that stopped at her toned thighs. The red six-inch heels added to her six-foot height, giving her the appearance of a runway goddess. The short, black, spiked hair contrasted the bright red lipstick that covered her small lips, but fitted her perfectly. *Damn!* BG thought as he eyed her.

The woman eyed BG in return. Smiling lasciviously at him, she batted her cold blue eyes at him and licked her lips. Her face was a mask of lust.

BG groped his slight erection and shook his head no. He'd never been into white chicks, but this one could sure *get it*... That is, if he wasn't madly in love with Monique. BG hit his alarm and climbed into his car. He could see the sexy-ass white chick slide into a red Lotus Evora S. He whipped out of the parking lot and saw that she was right behind him. *I know this hoe ain't stalkin' the kid*, he mused.

Jay-Z's *Lucky Me* played as he worked his way on to the expressway. It was late, so the expressway was relatively free of traffic. BG punched the BMW and coasted along. The red Lotus was still behind him. He was doing 85 mph. *I see that ma's really on a nigga,* he thought before switching lanes and gunning the BMW. He intended to lose her, but the Lotus changed lanes and sped up as well.

Okay, bitch, you wanna play? BG thought as he approached the exit. He was in the far lane, doing every bit of 105 mph. The Lotus was speeding along behind him. BG checked his rearview, seeing that the Lotus was the only car behind him, he snatched the steering wheel to the right and held it. The BMW veered across three lanes and barely missed the concrete barrier as it sailed down the off ramp.

Laughing to himself, BG caught the light and drove along the service road for a while, hoping that his stalker had gotten the point and gone on about her business. He got back on the expressway and continued towards home.

* * *

The automatic garage door lowered itself as BG snatched up the backpack and closed the door on the BMW. He was about to enter his home through the garage door when a sudden breath of cool air blew over him. It smelled of saltwater. *What the fuck?!* BG wondered where the breeze had come from, because there were no open windows in the garage and he lived nowhere near a beach. For some crazy reason he thought about the palm tree that he'd planted in his backyard less than a week ago. He had been told to check it every day. Sitting the backpack on the washing machine, BG exited the garage through the back door and walked along the rear of his house. *Goddamn!?!* he thought as he came to the palm tree. When he'd planted it, the small tree was knee-high. Now the

115

palm was up to his chest. BG couldn't believe his eyes. He'd never seen a tree grow so damned fast. And honestly, it scared him. The tree, digging up dead bodies, and casting spells, the whole ordeal gave BG the creeps. But it was for his man Haitian Jack, so he had to see it through. BG kneeled beside the palm tree and felt around the soil. *Nothing.* But then again, *nothing* was exactly what he had expected to find, because he had absolutely no faith in Voodoo.

BG brushed the dirt off of his hands and went inside.

Chapter 24

Both Mane and Mariah had showered and dressed. It was exactly eleven-thirty and Mane needed to begin his busy day – he had so much to do. All of the spots needed work, so he had to hurry and drop Mariah off; then cook, cut up, and bag up a kilo. He was guaranteed to be stuck in the *lay low* all day long, which was something that he hated. Mane loved nothing more than to be out and about; in the hood with his ROC niggas or bending corners in the Lambo, shitting on niggas. It was moments like this when he missed his subservient little white bitch the most, because he'd taught her everything about crack except how to use it – which she did not need to know. It would have been quick and easy for them to have gotten the work done together. *Together*, he thought, wondering if she was with someone else. The thought made him mad, so he pushed it aside. There were more important things that he needed to be thinking about.

Mariah kissed him, bringing him out of his lone contemplation. She smiled happily as he regarded her. Her lips were so soft. *And talented.* Mane blushed at the thought of what she'd done to him with those lips. From the time they'd left Wet Wetz and entered his small one room apartment it had been a nonstop, nonrestricted *fuckathon.* They swapped tongues, licked and sucked parts of one another that most people would be ashamed to mention.

"What's on your mind, baby?" she asked.

Mane shook his head. "Gotta lot to do."

"Well, did you enjoy yourself this time?"

Smiling, Mane kissed her. "I don't know if it was them *racks* you gave me or if you've been practicin'... But, Mariah, bitch, you got that fire!"

Mariah punched Mane in the chest. "Don't play, nigga! 'Cause I didn't *give* you shit. Remember that. I invested in us."

"Whatever," Mane said, grabbing his keys. "Let's go. I gotta get busy."

They walked out into the bright noon sun. Its rays beamed down on their skin.

"Damn, it's hot as hell out here." Mariah's pretty face was frowned.

"You done met the devil?" Mane asked as he locked the door.

"What?"

"I said —" Mane began, but his words caught in his throat as he spun around and saw the sleek black Nissan 370Z speeding up. "Aaaaaaaah, shit," he mumbled.

Mariah stared at the tall white girl that got out of the sports car. Her long black hair was braided to the back. Pink lipstick coated her lips. It matched her tight pink leather short-shorts and pink four-inch rhinestone heels. The white T-shirt was a V-neck with a big Playboy bunny outlined in pink rhinestones. The girl's huge titties were outlined beautifully against the thin material of the tight T-shirt. This was the first time that Mariah had ever wished that her breasts were bigger than they were. *Yeah, the bitch gotta lil' class,* Mariah admitted.

The girl, hands on hips, her pretty white face fixed in an angry scowl, looked from Mane to Mariah and back. Her voice cracked as she asked, "Who is this, Mane, your new girlfriend?!"

Mane shook his head and stuttered, "Umm, nah, this is... Ummm, this is Mariah. She, umm... We, you know..."

Mariah, though she was kind of pissed off at Mane for *sidelining* her for the white bitch, she really couldn't help but to laugh.

"And what's so fucking funny?!"

Mariah looked at the girl, surprised that she had the gall to confront her about a nigga – though she would've done the same thing had she been in the girl's shoes. She could see the hurt in her eyes, but hey, that was not her concern. "Mane," Mariah said, laughing some more. "You better get your lil' peoples."

"And if he doesn't?!"

"I'ma end up losin' one of my $300 heels in your lower-back, 'cause bitch, you ain't got no ass!" Mariah said with boss bitch assurance. "Now keep tryin' me, cracka."

Red-faced and fuming, the girl started towards Mariah, but Mane quickly stepped in front of her, easily stopping her from walking over in Mariah's space; because truthfully, the girl really did not want any problems with Mariah. She was just hurt and angry, which gave way to foolish actions that were dictated by her ego and pride.

"No!" she yelled, snatching away from Mane. "Don't fucking touch me! Don't ever touch me again! Because I hate your ass!"

"Lina, hold up," Mane tried to say.

"No," she said, this time calmer. Tears were running down her sad face. Her body shook as she spoke. "I knew that you were fucking around on me. But I didn't care because I loved you... I thought that I needed you... But you know what, fuck you, Mane... Just fuck you," she said before jumping in her car and speeding off.

"Damn!" Mane said and walked past Mariah, who stood laughing. Mane got in the Lambo and fired up the engine. He really wanted to ride off after his girl, but he had to take Mariah home.

Damn, Mane, you really fucked up this time... I told your stupid-ass to take the bitch to a motel, but nah, you had to bring her to the lay low, Mane's conscience scolded him.

Mariah got in the car and looked over at Mane. A wicked little smile spread across her face. "So, umm, I guess that was your lil' peoples, huh?" She laughed.

Mane pulled out of the yard and turned towards 14th Avenue. "What's so damn funny?" he asked, visibly irritated.

"*Ppsstt!* You can sit over there and act like you're mad all you want to, but you're too funny! You and your lil' girlfriend... *Hmp!* I'm the one that should be pissed-ass off," she fussed.

Mane turned onto 103rd Street and asked, "Mad for what?"

"Boy, you might've tried me... I can't believe you had me, Miss Mariah, comin' off the bench for that tired-ass white bitch... Nooo," she said and laughed some more. "Then had the nerve to holla at me 'bout *your lady gotta have something.* Well, after seein' her, it's obvious you wasn't talkin' 'bout ass, 'cause *Snow White* is in the negative, honey."

"Shut up," Mane said coolly.

Yo Gotti's *Respect That You Earn* played through the Lambo's system.

They rode the entire fifteen minute ride without saying anything further.

Mane whipped up into her driveway and put the car in park.

Mariah cut her sexy brown eyes over at him. He wasn't a pretty nigga, but something about him just did it for her. Mariah was a dime and could have just about any nigga that she wanted, but for whatever reason she'd found it in her heart to choose Mane. "So, umm, I understand you're a lil' busy or whatever and you've gotta few *people problems*, but when I'ma see you again?"

"I don't know," Mane answered.

"Well, your lil' ass better figure it out, nigga."

"Whatever, girl."

"Okay, think I'm playin' with you, boy," Mariah said, frowning up her pretty face.

"Bye, Mariah."

"Give me a kiss."

"Bye."

"Look, I'ma probably have to go outta town for a day or two, so get it together while I'm gone." Mariah leaned over and tongue-kissed Mane.

He kissed her back.

Smiling brightly, Mariah got out of the expensive sports car and shook her juicy ass extra hard as she walked off towards the front door.

Mane watched her closely. He loved her ass. But he wasn't in love with her. He waited until she was inside of her house before he pulled off, his ex-girlfriend heavy on his mind...

Chapter 25

Gemo pushed the Range Rover through the eleven o'clock traffic. King sat on the passenger side of the exorbitant SUV, bobbing his head to Plies' *Rich Folks* as they rode along. A thick cloud of smoke hung in the closed space; evidence of the high-powered blunt of *Killer* that they'd smoked after dropping off the two white chicks that they'd picked up in Wet Wetz. They'd had a real blast swinging with the two white sluts, but as Gemo looked at all of the missed calls on his cell phone from Danielle, his forever wifey, he wasn't sure if the *off the chain* sex with the white bitches was worth it.

"Say, Gemo, what did BG say?" King asked, breaking Gemo's train of thought.

Gemo cut his eyes at King. "He said he couldn't do nothing with the two million. So we gotta keep doin' us."

"We need that *clean*... Dog, that lil' five bricks that we copped from your people in A-Town ain't gonna last a nigga no time," King bemoaned. "For real, dog, your lil' cousin's a real fuck-nigga. A pussy-boy to the heart! And I told you that from the jump. That bitch-ass nigga don't wanna see you on top, he want you under him. And that's fucked up! 'Specially after you raised the lil' nigga, gave him a plug that he robbed, killed, and got rich off of... Then, then, my nigga, the pussy-nigga got your hoe killed! Nah, Gemo, dog, that nigga owe you, and he ain't playin' fair... But you already know that, just like you knew that shit wasn't gonna work last night."

Gemo started to check King about the disrespectful names he'd placed on BG, but decided against it because King was partly right. BG was playing it *raw.* He had all that free cocaine, cocaine that had cost Gemo his little cousin LG, his girl Black Barbie, and his plug; yet BG wouldn't sell him one hundred funky-ass kilos. True enough, Gemo had lied about the $19,500 a piece offer from his people in Atlanta in an attempt to get BG to beat the offer, but it wasn't like Gemo was coming begging. He had $2,000,000 to spend and his people in Atlanta couldn't handle an order that big. They'd only been able to scrape up five or six at a time, which they charged him $26,500 apiece. But Gemo couldn't complain because the work was clean and it beat the $36,000 that King's people in Miami was charging – and King's people were selling whacked up trash. No, he couldn't check King, that would've been foul, because BG was the one that needed checking.

"Did you pay the lil' broad?" Gemo asked King.

"Hell nah, I ain't give that white bitch nothing!" King replied.

Gemo sucked his teeth and shook his head. "Maaan, I'm not talkin' 'bout that stank-ass bitch! I'm talkin' 'bout the lil' red broad that be runnin' to A-Town for us."

"Oh, yeah, I paid the bitch."

Gemo nodded. "If my man hit me back today, you think she'll be ready to ride?"

"I don't know, but we can damn sure ride by there and see."

Checking his rearview and side mirrors, Gemo switched lanes and set his course for the chick's house. They were only about ten minutes away. Gemo picked up his cell phone and tried his people in Atlanta as they rode, because the spot in Little Haiti was pumping and he did not want to run out of product or be forced to have to buy the garbage that King's people was pushing.

Gemo turned on to the chick's street and slowed to turn into her driveway, but King stopped him.

"Nah, keep goin', keep goin'!" King yelled.

Gemo glanced and saw the extravagant traveling apparatus and knew immediately who it belonged to. He sped off and backed into a driveway three houses down. Watching. The flawless red-bone soon got out of the car and sashayed off towards her front door. Gemo admired her perfect ass and hips. *Damn, that's a bad lil' bitch there!* he thought as she disappeared into the house.

The car zoomed past.

Gemo allowed it some space before he pulled out to pursue it...

Chapter 26

The full moon shone through the upstairs windows of the two-story house. A strong breeze, warm and spirited, whisked the dark curtains that hung open. Candles flickered. Papa C sipped a pungent brew of herbs and sugar cane liquor as he watched Papa Guede draw the veve of Legba, the gatekeeper of the spiritual realm. The veve was outlined with corn flour, in the center of the large room, encircled by flickering candles and salt. Once this was done Papa Guede, the dark priest from Haiti, thanked Legba for opening the door to his realm and begged the mighty gatekeeper for protection and strength.

As he mumbled and rocked back and forth, a faint crack of lightning sounded. The warm breeze began blowing harder. Papa C watched in awe as Papa Guede placed Duke's decayed remains in the center of the circle. The clothes that Papa C had taken from Judge Anderson were used to dress the cadaver. Papa Guede lifted a wooden bowl from the floor and began drinking the strong brew – a mixture of blood, sugar cane liquor and twenty-one caustic herbs. All that wasn't consumed, he poured into his eyes and started shaking a small rattle. Mumbling. He stared into space, positioned east of the circle, because the spirit was due to approach from the west… The chanting grew louder. The thunder claps came in greater frequency.

"Let my enemies, who speak against Haitian Jack, cease to speak, lose sleep, cease to think on their own accord... Make their mouths speak as I say... Haitian Jack is still, but I say free, free, free, free!!!" the old Haitian man yelled in his native tongue.

He continued to chant this until finally he fell into a trance, losing all mastery over his body. His eyes rolled and he started shaking uncontrollably before falling unconscious. For three and one-half minutes he lay, unbreathing. Dead. Then the loa entered his body. Papa Guede rose. Stared blankly.

Three black dogs, three black cats, and three chickens had been slaughtered for the invocation, their blood kept in a bucket. Papa C poured a generous amount of Haitian rum into Papa Guede's wooden bowl and took it to him, along with a big cigar and the big platter of rotting, raw animal flesh. And as the possessed Voodoo priest began eating, drinking, and smoking, Papa C used the animal blood to paint the necessary veves and splash the white walls of the dark room. Sweat leathered his dark body as he worked. He could feel the spirits at work, smell the presence of the petro loa. At times, he himself was almost overwhelmed by the existing evil... Silently. Sincerely. He thanked the demons that he served and begged them for protection and continued prosperity...

Chapter 27

BG stood behind the bar at Wet Wetz with two of his best waitresses. He was personally training them to run the bar because he could not stand the long hours any longer. It seemed he'd just laid down when his alarm clock woke him. That was at nine o'clock that morning. It was now going on eleven o'clock and he felt as if he was sleepwalking. He was dead tired. Through tired eyes, he watched the influx of traffic stream into the semi-packed club. Something caught his attention. Black leather and high heels. The tight leather pants and halter blouse augmented the woman's long, shapely body. Her pale skin glowed against the dark material and her short black hair, which was gelled straight back. Black lipstick, blue eyes. It was the coquette from last night. Again she batted those eyes at him and licked her sensuous lips. BG blinked and looked away. *Am I trippin'?* he wondered. He'd read somewhere that the body did not function properly when weary. *I gotta get outta here and get some rest,* he told himself, but before he could move she was standing directly in front of him at the bar.

"Hello," she whispered, her voice husky. She had a thick accent that was foreign to him.

"Oh, what's up?" BG returned as he stared into her smiling face. Her features were chiseled, sort of hard, but feminine enough to stir his desires. She looked exactly like the beautiful Ireland Baldwin.

"A *Wet Wet*, please," she said, her blue eyes bore into his, as if searching his soul.

Something about her made him nervous. BG looked away. Then he whispered something to one of the girls he'd been training and quickly exited through the back. Subconsciously he rubbed at the thin, sturdy material that covered his chest. *Man, I'm trippin'*, he thought and slid into his BMW. He was zipping out of the parking lot when his cell phone rang.

"Yeah," he answered and listened to Mane rattle off a string of excited gibberish, most of which made no sense to him. "Hold on, say that shit again, but slow down."

He listened as he drove. Frowned. Suddenly he saw red.

"What?!" BG finally exclaimed. "Look, I'm on my way, so don't move and don't touch shit!" BG hung up and floored the gas pedal. He was no longer paying attention to his surroundings, he was just driving, recklessly, with no regard for his safety. Anger had replaced his wariness. And in less than fifteen minutes he was standing beside Mane in the little one room *lay low*. The place had been thoroughly tossed. *Hurricaned*. The dresser drawers had been pulled out, mattress flipped, carpet pulled up. Mane's clothes and personal effects were thrown all over the floor. Someone had broke in and tore the spot up.

BG shook his head. "What did they hit you for?"

Mane was so mad that he had tears running down his dark-brown face. "Six bricks... 'Bout sixty stacks and some of my jewelry," he croaked softly.

BG felt bad for his little man. "Was that everything?"

Shaking his head no, Mane replied, "Nah, I got like one hun'ed at the house and probably 'bout thirty in the streets... But, bruh, somebody tried me, bruh, and I'ma kill them when I find out who. I don't give a fuck who they are, they're dead, bruh... Dead!"

"Nah, lil' nigga, *you* ain't gon' kill them," BG said coolly. *"We're* gon' kill them... And I swear on everything..."

"When I leave this earth, it's gon' be on both feet..."

BG smiled. "Never knees in the dirt... You can try me, muthafucka, but when I squeeze it hurts..."

"Fine, we'll lose two lives, yours and mine... Give me any amount of time, don't let my ROC niggas grieve..."

"In the funeral home cryin', droppin' tears on my sleeve... You feel me?" BG finished.

Mane nodded. "I hear you, bruh."

"Nah, lil' nigga, fuck that! Do you feel me?"

"Yeah, I feel you." He gave BG some dap.

The two sat down on two chairs.

BG pulled out a pre-rolled blunt of 'dro. Lit it. Hit it twice and passed it to Mane. The two sat quiet, smoking and thinking. Bemused. Somebody had disrespected them. But who?! The longer they sat thinking the more enraged they became. Of course, BG knew that they would have to allow the initial wave of anger to subside before they could effectively move out, because acting on emotions would only lead them to move foolishly. And he was nobody's fool.

"Man, tell me this," BG finally said. "Who all knew where this *lay low* was?"

"Huh?"

"Boy, if your ass can *huh* you can hear."

Looking crazy, Mane asked, "Like, umm, includin' you?"

"Lil' nigga, don't play with me!" BG stared at Mane hard. "Besides me."

"Oh, umm, maybe like..." Mane furrowed his brow as he thought, knowing already that he'd fucked up, because *nobody* was supposed to know about the *lay low*. "Maybe 'bout two people."

BG shook his head sadly. "And that's two too many... Boy, don't you know it ain't a *lay low* no more once somebody knows where it's at?! Your *lay low* is safety! And it's only safe because it's secret."

Mane did not say anything. He just sat looking stupid, because that's all he could do until he found out who had robbed him. He'd slipped and somebody had gripped.

"Was it two hoes?"

"BG, big homie, I don't know. When I got here the —"

"Boy, not who broke in! I'm talkin' 'bout the two muthafuckas that you brought here!" BG was getting upset now. *The more I teach this lil' nigga it seems the dumber he gets*, he mused.

"Oh, my bad, big homie... But yeah, it was two hoes," Mane answered.

"Who?"

"My lil' chick Mariah and..." Mane paused, he did not want to lie to BG but he could not betray his girlfriend's trust — even though she'd cursed him out and dismissed him. "...umm, I don't know the other chick's name. She was just a lil' *jump off* that I seen walkin' past the spot one day. I was on pills and just slipped, bruh," Mane lied.

Again BG shook his head sadly. He'd once been young himself, but he did not remember being as careless as Mane. "Well, if it was her, that lil' *jump off* was an expensive one."

Mane nodded his agreement.

BG continued. "I'ma get Tony to check the spot out, so fix the door and get me the new key. And don't bring —" BG stopped and thought. "In fact, don't come 'round here no more 'til I say so."

"Aiight, I'll call the people now."

"Do that," BG agreed. "We're gon' lay on that bitch Mariah and see what's up with her."

"When?"

"Later. I'ma call you." BG stood up and began his exit, but stopped as he stepped out of the door. He turned around and faced Mane. Angrily, he said, "And get rid of that muthafuckin' car! Not tomorrow or tonight, but today! If I come back 'round here or see that damn Lambo again I'ma blow that shit up! And you're gonna owe them crackas at Prestige a whole lotta money that you ain't got. Now think I'm playin'!"

Mane nodded his head and BG left.

Chapter 28

Tony Galletta eased his big six-foot-three frame into the unmarked Chevy Impala and set out for Little River. He'd finally gotten some free time away from the murder case involving the Hungarian mob boss, Andras Simonyi, which was going absolutely nowhere, and decided that he would go ahead and handle the small favor that BG had asked of him two days ago.

As Tony navigated the Impala his mind turned over the circumstances concerning the Simonyi murder case. No prints, no witnesses, and seemingly no clear motive. A hit from within the Hungarian Mafia? Had Andras been clipped by an outside faction for maybe stepping on someone else's toes? And where was the computer modular that ran the security cameras? Had the suspects taken it to cover themselves or had Andras' associates gotten to it first and planned to do their own investigation? *God help the guys that killed Andras if those damn Hungarians have that computer modular*, Tony mused as he pulled up to the rear efficiency. He got out and looked around before getting the burglary kit he'd taken from the station and the door key that BG had given him.

Tony entered the small one room apartment and looked around. The place was a mess. Stuffy. He put the kit down and hit the fridge. Empty except for two bottles of Tiger's Root beer. Tony belched loudly after drinking them both and then began looking the place over.

Clothes. More clothes. The big plasma TV was still in place and so was the sound system. *Well, at least they weren't petty thieves,* he mused. Spotting a picture on the floor, near the bed, he kneeled down and picked it up. A naked chick. Young. But fine as hell. Tony searched around and found a stack of nude pictures. Spanish chicks. Thick red-bones. Sexy black babies. There was ever a white chick. Kind of thin, but sexy. Tony frowned because the white chick's face was covered on each shot of her. *Gotta give it to Mane, by God, he's a real magnet for the honeys*, he thought before placing the pictures neatly under the mattress.

The entry was through the front door – the only door the little place had. A crowbar, he figured from the looks of the doorjamb. Tony opened the burglary kit and began the tedious task of finger dusting the apartment for prints. The refrigerator handle, knobs on the dresser drawers, cabinet handles, and all flat surfaces that a person searching an apartment might carelessly touch. When he finally finished, he'd worked up a nice little sweat and two long hours had passed.

Well, he thought, wiping his sweaty neck and face with a clean white handkerchief, *I guess that about does it, I'd say.*

Tony took another long look at Mane's stack of naked *chick-flicks*, locked the place up, and was on his way. He would place the prints he had lifted and run them through the computer for matches as soon as he got another free day.

Chapter 29

BG sat behind his huge oak desk in the spacious upstairs office that he had in Club Wet Wetz. Across from him sat Monique, their accountant, and a corporate lawyer that they both used regularly for business purposes. They had been cooped up in the office for the last three or four hours going over the necessary paperwork to protect both BG and Monique in the event their marriage went sour, or worst, if BG was indicted.

Looking at his G Shock, BG saw that it was exactly twelve-twenty. He sighed. "Look, I trust Monique, if I didn't I wouldn't be marrying her. She's the mother of my two sons and I have more money than I'll ever need, so I'm not trippin' y'all. I just wanna protect her money from the crackas if I get jammed up, that's it, I'm not worried 'bout nothing else."

The two white men were used to BG using the word *cracka* around them and they took no offense. They knew that the usage was in reference to the *powers that be*.

"I agree," Monique said. "I love and trust BG. Besides, he has more money than I'll ever make in this lifetime." She remembered the big boxes of money that he had shown her.

"Understood. Still, we must get this signed before the wedding, which is fast approaching. I know that you both love and trust one another, but so did the last twenty couples that I've represented in divorce court," the lawyer stated.

The accountant nodded his agreement.

They haggled on for another thirty minutes before the papers were signed and the lawyer left.

BG then turned to the accountant. "Okay, that shit's over... Now, when can I spend some money?"

Sighing, the accountant flipped through his books. BG's bottom-line was very impressive. Wet Wetz was a literal gold mine. Of course, he understood that drug money was being washed through the bar. Pouring over the figures a bit longer, he said, "With the expenses for the wedding and honeymoon set aside, I figure you can spend about $125,000, give or take a few grand."

BG nodded, but before he could respond a knock sounded at his office door. "Hold that thought," he said and walked to the door. Opening it, he found Danielle standing there. She'd shed a few pounds and was looking damn good. "Damn, sis, what it do?!"

Danielle forced a smile. The two embraced. "I'm okay, BG, but I really need to talk to you if you're not too busy."

BG turned to Monique and the account. "Yo, give me a few, I'll be right back."

They both nodded and BG walked off with Danielle at his side.

The club was jam packed.

Wale's *Vanity* played loudly as BG found a spot at the bar for them to sit. He then ordered two glasses of red wine and waited for Danielle to open up the dialogue. It had been a long time since he'd seen her. Now, being there with her at the bar, two glasses of red wine between them, it felt a bit awkward.

Danielle looked around the large club at the strange cultural mix that BG had managed to create with Wet Wetz. A few upper-middle class blacks, wild Hispanics, and a bunch of rich whites. Ranging from ages eighteen to thirty-five, they were all there in Wet Wetz partying together.

Finally, Danielle looked at BG and cleared her throat. "Well, I guess you know why I'm here?"

"To tell me that you've finally decided to leave big cuz for me," he said, smiling.

Danielle laughed and playfully slapped the back of his hand. "No, crazy." She paused, looked at him seriously. "But, BG, I am leavin' your cousin."

BG was shocked to hear that. "Why, what's up?"

She shook her head. Sipped her wine. A tear played at the corner of her sad eyes, but she wiped it away before it could run down her smooth brown face. "I just can't do it anymore... I've put up with the other women, the time away in prison, the nights out hustlin', but nothing's changin'. Nothing! He talked about doin' better, leavin' the women and all that street mess alone, but nothing has changed..." She laughed to herself. "I actually came here tonight to see him, to talk about our situation, but the young lady runnin' the bar says that Gemo hasn't worked here for a month now, and he's been leavin' home early and comin' home in the wee-hours, lyin' to me, like he still worked here."

BG just shook his head. What could he say. "But you know he loves you right?"

Danielle laughed. "No, BG, I don't... And truthfully, neither does he. Because if he did he would not do the things that he does. No, if he loved me he would not risk goin' back to prison or bein' killed in those streets and bein' taken away from me!" Danielle wiped away more tears. "I have two sons, BG, that I love, and I can't risk their lives and well-bein' for Gemo anymore. They need me! And I can't allow myself to possibly contract AIDS or get drug into a situation that'll take me away from them. No, those days are over... It hurts, BG, but I have to move on."

BG felt her. She was dead right. Her words even made him consider his own situation. Was Monique thinking the same way about him? "Listen, Danielle, you and Gemo have been together for too long to just walk away like this. I mean, kid has his faults, but he really does love you. He..."

136

"No." Danielle shook her head. "Don't waste your time... I didn't come by here for that. It's been too long and too much has happened. I'ma grown woman and I have to act accordingly." She drunk the rest of her wine, forced another smile. "I just wanted you to know that I tried and I wanted to thank you for all that you've given me."

"Damn, you act like it's over between us! I thought you was leavin' Gemo, not me."

Danielle laughed. She hugged him. Placed a wet kiss on his lips. "Never that, BG... I'll always be your friend."

"And I'll always be yours."

"Good."

He nodded. BG felt so bad for her. She'd given Gemo so much of herself. "Don't hesitate to call me for anything, Danielle, I got you."

Danielle flashed that faint smile and turned to leave before she broke down crying.

Chapter 30

The digital clock on the gold Aston Martin DB5 read twelve-thirty. Meek Mill's *Who Your Around* featuring Mary J. Blige, played loudly as Mane drove the expensive car up 103rd Street. Sadam was on the passenger side, sparking a blunt of 'dro. The two young thugs had been on pills, 'dro and Moet all day. Vibing. Shopping. Showing the streets that the robbery had not hurt him – fronting for real, because the robbery had hurt him, but he could not let them know it. Following BG's orders, Mane had returned the Gallardo to Prestige, but had left the exotic rental car lot with the gold Aston Martin DB5. He'd also bought two big rose-gold Cuban-links with diamond infested medallions. *Can't never let up on these streets*, he thought. *Reputation is everything out here and you gotta always protect it!*

Whipping the Aston Martin up into Wet Wetz, he snatched the Gucci backpack up and hit the alarm. Sadam followed him through the club's entrance and into the sea of dancing bodies. Chris Brown's *Strip* was playing. As they approached the bar, Mane spotted BG hugging a thick brown-skinned chick. The chick then turned and began walking away. She looked sad, on the verge of tears. Passing her, Mane hit the Big Gangsta with a crisp salute. BG returned the salute.

"What's up?"

"Same shit, different day."

"You hear anything?"

"Not really, but the bitch's back in town."

BG nodded. "You seen her?"

"Nah. The bitch called me 'bout thirty minutes ago."

"We'll check her out tomorrow." BG looked at the red dude, Sadam, and could easily see that he was high as hell, which meant that Mane was probably high also. "Yo, come upstairs," BG told Mane as he walked off.

"Get us some bottles, kid, I'll be right back," Mane told Sadam and followed BG upstairs to his private office. Upon entering the spacious, well decorated office, Mane was surprised to find Monique sitting beside BG's desk talking to the white accountant. He spoke to them and sat down on the over-stuffed leather couch that sat next to the big two-way glass window that overlooked the club below. He could see the entire club from where he sat.

BG took his position behind the big desk and began talking. Mane could hear BG saying whatever it was he was saying, but he wasn't sure if BG was talking to him, Monique or the accountant. Mane's mind was elsewhere. He did not come to the club for a lecture or financial advice. He simply wanted to give BG the $100,000 that he had in the Gucci backpack, drink a few bottles, and hopefully do some *shoning*. That's it, that's all. He was still peering out of the two-way glass into the crowded club when he spotted her. She was dressed in a short black skirt, white sheer top, and long high-heeled riding boots. Mane watched her, laughing and flirting with some tall Spanish guy. The two of them went to the bar and downed two drinks before hitting the dance floor.

This pussy-ass bitch! Mane thought as he watched the two *dirty-dance*. The dude was all over her, his hand caressing the inside of her thigh. Mane fought to control his anger, but easily loss the battle. He stood up and made for the door.

"Hey, yo, Mane, what's good?!" BG asked, surprised by Mane's sudden departure.

Without looking back or breaking his stride, Mane said over his shoulder, "That's $100,000 in the backpack, I'll holla at you in the mornin', bruh."

When Mane made it downstairs, he waved Sadam over. The young hoodlum got up and followed Mane to the crowded dance floor. The two elbowed and pushed their way through the horde of frolicking bodies — all fantastically tripping to the array of colorful lights and fast blends of Hip Hop and Techno music.

Mane, finally finding himself beside the couple, slapped the dude's hand off of the chick's thigh.

"Hey, what's your —"

Sadam cut the Spanish dude's protest off with a straight right to the mouth. Seeing that there was two of them, the dude covered his bleeding mouth with both hands and disappeared in the crowd.

The chick looked at Mane, her face registering surprise. Mane could also see that she was high on pills. He grabbed her arm and pulled her through the crowd, towards the exit. She tried to pull away, but Mane's grip was too strong.

"You're hurting my fucking arm! Let go!" she yelled.

"I'ma be hurtin' more than your arm if you don't shut the fuck up and come on!"

"You don't tell me what to do anymore! You don't own me, Mane! So get your dirty hands off of me!"

Mane stopped. And before she knew it, he had slapped the hell out of her. "Now shut the fuck up!"

She began crying as Mane pulled her outside.

Sadam was right behind them.

"Where the fuck is your car, bitch?!" Mane asked the crying female.

"Over, over there." She pointed.

"Give me the keys!"

She went in the small purse that was draped over her shoulder and handed the keys to Mane.

"My nigga, drive this shit home. I'ma holla at you in the morning." Mane pushed the girl into the Aston Martin DB5, got in himself and peeled out. He was so distracted, angry and high off pills, he never noticed the red Lotus following him as he sped out of the parking lot.

Still crying, the girl sat with her hand covering her face.

Mane cut his eyes at her as he sped through traffic. "You think I'm pussy, huh?!"

She ignored him.

"Lina, bitch, I know you hear me!"

"Just, leave me alone, okay... You embarrassed me in front of all these people! You ruined my whole night, Mane... I hate you," she cried.

"Bitch, I embarrassed you?! Nah, you embarrassed your muthafuckin' self! And stupid bitch, you embarrassed me! You s'posed to be my hoe, but you're all out in public, high on pills, with a nigga's hand all up your skirt. Hoe, you might've really tried me."

"Well, fuck you, Mane. Because I'm not your hoe!"

Mane sucked his teeth. "Bitch, you're crazy. You're gonna be mine for forever... Lina, can't you see that I love you?! I've been callin' your fuckin' phone every day tryna holla at you! You know why? Huh? It's 'cause a nigga's been sick without you, that's why," Mane confessed.

She wanted to believe him, because truthfully, she still loved him, too. But he'd hurt her. "You don't love me, liar... You only love yourself... If you loved me you wouldn't have had that girl at your house."

Before Mane could respond he noticed something in his rearview mirror. A car was following him. *Aaaaaah, fuck! Just what I needed*, Mane thought as the red and blue lights came on. "Fuck!"

Mane said aloud and pulled over. His gun was in the hidden stash spot and he'd given all of the pills and weed to Sadam before they'd left for the club.

The cop approached the car, hand on his gun. "Hands on the wheel, where I can see them," he said, peeking into the car. He saw that it was a couple. "This your car, son?"

Mane shook his head. "No, sir... belongs to the label."

"Label?"

"Yes, sir, BadLand Music. I'm a rapper," Mane lied with a straight face.

No, you're a goddamn liar! his girlfriend thought, wanting to laugh at his ass.

"Is that so?"

"Yes, sir, it's true. We just left my album release party."

The white cop eyed Mane. The kid did look like a rapper. "License and registration."

Mane passed the officer his driver's license and the car's registration papers.

The officer walked back to his car. He called in Mane's name. And he also called in for a female officer to come out. Mane's name came back clean. Ten minutes later the second unit arrived. The female officer got out and they approached the car.

"Here's your paperwork, young man. But we're gonna need the two of you to step out of the car for a quick search and you can be on your way," the male policeman explained.

Mane sucked his teeth, but he got out of the car.

"You too, Miss," the policewoman said.

When they were both out of the car, the male officer shined his flashlight through the car. Looked under the seat and turned to Mane for a *pat-down*. Mane was clean.

The policewoman patted Mane's girlfriend down. "Mind if I look in your purse?" she asked the girl.

"I don't care," the girl snapped, but it was not until after the words had left her mouth that she remembered the pills. *Aaaaaah, fuck, noooo,* she thought, hoping the officer would not find them.

"Oh," the policewoman said, pulling out a clear baggie of red pills – eight pills in total. "And what are these?"

Mane's eyes bucked. *What the fuck?!* he thought, knowing exactly what they were – *Red Monkeys.*

The girl was quickly handcuffed and driven away.

Mane jumped in the car and followed the police. He could not believe that his girl was going to jail for possession. Lifting his cell phone, he called his bondsman. He knew that the bondsman was going to be pissed at him for calling at this hour, but Mane did not care – he needed his girl out right away.

"Hello?" the sleepy voice answered.

"Yeah, Randy, it's Mane."

"What do you want, Mane?" He was clearly upset.

"I need you to raise my people."

The man sighed. "What's the charge?"

"Possession."

"Name?"

"Angelina Galletta."

"I'll call you," Randy said and hung up.

FOUR HOURS LATER

Angelina was so pissed. Humiliated. She'd never been treated so bad in her life. The women CO's had forced her to strip, spread her vagina and butt open, and allow them to stick their fingers inside of her. Angelina felt dirty and violated as she exited the county jail. Last night had no doubt been the absolute worst day of her young life. But at least she was out. Another few hours in that sordid, roach infested building would have driven her insane. Of course, the worst was not over. Angelina knew that her father was going to kill her when he found out that she'd been arrested for possession of *ecstasy.*

I am so done, she thought as she walked. It was morning, six o'clock. *If I never see a pill again that'll be too soon*, Angelina mused.

Hearing someone call her name, she looked and saw Mane waving her over. A deeper frown instantly spread across her face. It was all his fault. She walked over, got into the Aston Martin, and slammed the door shut without so much as looking at him.

"You aiight?" Mane asked her as he pulled the car into the early morning traffic.

She did not utter one word. Angelina just wanted to get to her car so that she could go home, take a long hot bath, and go to sleep. Maybe then she would wake up and this terrible ordeal would have gone away — remembered only as a bad dream.

"Well, are you hungry?" Mane asked.

Angelina sucked her teeth and rolled her tired eyes. "No, okay. No, no, no! I just want my car, okay?! Take me to my car and please just leave me alone."

Mane wanted to slap her ass, but he realized that she was not herself. She had been through a lot over the past five hours. "Look, Lina, I'm sorry, aiight... But you gotta work with me if we're gonna fix this."

"Fix what?!"

"Our relationship."

"*Ppsstt!* We no longer have a *relationship*, thanks to you."

"Thanks to me, huh?!" Mane asked, feeling his anger returning. "You was just in my big homie's club, runnin' wild like a *pill-animal*... Had nigga's hands all up in your pussy, but everything's my fault, huh?!"

"I caught you with that girl!"

"Yeah, after you left me!"

"No, after you ran me away with your bullshit lies!" She was crying again.

He sighed. "I didn't lie! I was with BG that night! We went out to the graveyard —"

"Yeah, yeah, Mane, you told me, and dug up a dead body." She laughed.

"Okay, Lina, I was with a bitch... Is that what you wanna hear?! I was with the bitch Mariah that you caught me with the other morning. You happy now?"

"Yes, I'm happy now, because at least I know the *truth*!"

Mane shook his head sadly. "You know the truth now..."

Angelina cried. She wanted to hate him so bad, but the truth was, she loved him too much. "You should've just told me the truth, Mane... That's all you had to do."

But he had told her the truth, and she'd rejected it, instead having clung on to a lie. "Well, I'm sorry, Lina, and it'll never happen again, 'cause I really do love you... A nigga ain't perfect, baby, but I'ma do my best to make things right. I promise."

She nodded and wiped her tear-streaked face...

Chapter 31

TWENTY-FOUR HOURS LATER

BG sat behind the wheel of the old service van. Mane sat on the passenger seat and Sadam sat behind them on the first row of bench seats. They had been parked across from Mariah's house for the past two hours. Her black Lexus IS 350 was parked in its space. A gray Range Rover was parked beside it. That bothered BG, because he thought he knew whose Range Rover that was. *But it's a lot of gray Range Rovers in Dade County*, he told himself. But all doubts were eradicated when a forest-green BMW whipped up behind the Range Rover and a tall, skinny Haitian man jumped out. It was King. The trio watched as the door opened. Mariah, very pretty and fine as ever, frowned at King before stepping aside and letting him in.

"What's up," Mane asked, seeing the confused look on BG's face.

"Nothin," BG replied.

A cell phone rung before anything further could be said. BG answered, "Yeah?"

"Where are you?"

"Ridin'."

"Need to see you."

"When?"

"Now."

BG wanted to hang around and see what he could see, but he knew that this had to be important. "Okay, where?"

"How about that lake on 99th Street and 12th?"

Hobo Land, BG thought. "Aiight, cool. I'm on my way now."

"Good. See you in a few."

They both hung up.

* * *

"'Bout muthafuckin' time you got here!" Gemo said as King entered the spacious den. He had been there since early that morning shifting and mixing the heroin and cocaine for the trap. Their spot was *booming*. Business had picked up one hundred percent since Gemo had gotten involved with the trap. The product was now *cleaner* and the bags were fatter.

"Aye, boy, something goin' on!" King said nervously.

"Here we go again." Gemo shook his head, because King always came with some bullshit whenever he was *out of pocket*, when all the nigga had to do was admit that he'd been somewhere goofing off.

"Nah, kid, I'm for real!" King lit a Newport and pulled it hard.

"Ut'un, nigga! I told your ass not to smoke in my house!" Mariah fussed. She did not like King. He was suspect in her book. She'd been going out of town for them and letting them *sack up* their drugs in her house from time to time because of her relationship with Gemo. She admired and respected Gemo. He was about seven years older than her, but he had always treated her good.

"My bad," King said, dropping the lit cigarette on her tile floor and smashing it out with his Bally shoe.

Mariah rolled her eyes. She knew that King's ugly-ass was just being nasty, but that was okay, because she would not have to deal with his ass much longer. With the money she was making going out of town and letting them use her house, she'd be able to pay off her car, put up a few dollars and hit Mane off with a big lump sum of cash. She really liked Mane and she knew that he would do right by her on the financial tip, even if their personal relationship never became exclusive like she wanted it to be.

"Gemo, kid, somebody's been followin' me since yesterday," King stated.

"Followin' you?"

"Yeah. A cracka in a red Lotus."

Gemo frowned. "Kid, ain't no police gon' be in no red Lotus followin' no nigga."

King lit another Newport. "Nigga, I ain't said nothing 'bout no police! I said a cracka in a Lotus was followin' me... And, nigga, it's a white van with tints on it parked across the street, so somebody's followin' your ass, too!"

"What?!"

"Yeah, nigga, the van was there when I just pulled up."

Gemo jumped up from the table and raced to the window. Slowly he pulled the curtain back. Nothing. "Nigga, you're gookin'! Ain't no muthafuckin' van out there."

King pushed him aside. "Let me see!" He looked. The van was gone. *What the fuck?* he thought as he turned to face Gemo. "Dog, I'm tellin' you, it was out there when I pulled up."

"Yeah, just like the police was followin' you in a red Lotus." Gemo went back into the den. "Nigga, come help me finish sackin' up this shit so we can go."

* * *

Hobo Land was a wooded area that sat in the middle of the neighborhood. It was rumored to have alligators in the big lake, but that never stopped the neighborhood children from fishing and swimming in the lake.

BG stood looking into the dirty water. He could see shopping carts and automobiles in the lake. He could imagine there being dead bodies down there. His mind was drawn from the lake by the sound of an approaching car. He looked and saw Tony's unmarked Chevy turn into the sandy field that fronted the lake.

The big six-foot-three, 300 pound Italian climbed out of the car and walked right over to Mane and Sadam. And without warning, he punched Mane square in the face. The blow sent Mane flying to the ground.

Sadam yanked his .9mm.

And so did Tony.

BG ran over and stood between the two weapons. "Aye, man, what the fuck are y'all doin'?!" BG exclaimed.

Ignoring BG, Tony frowned down at Mane, who was laying there holding his bleeding mouth. "You fuckin' my daughter, you little punk?!" When Tony had ran the prints that he'd lifted from Mane's apartment earlier that morning, Angelina Galletta had popped up, showing that she'd been arrested the day before for possession of ecstasy. He'd then remembered the naked pictures of the white girl he'd seen in the apartment. "You got her doin' drugs and goin' to jail, you little punk!"

"Wait a minute, Tony," BG said, holding the big Italian back. "Mane, you fuckin' this man's daughter?"

Mane just dropped his head.

"I ought to fuckin' kill him!" Tony said, trying to raise his gun, but BG held his arm down to his side. "She's only eighteen, you fuckin' punk!"

"Come on, Tony, Mane's only twenty... So it's not really a big deal —"

"Not a big deal?!" Tony looked at BG, frowning. "I'm a fuckin' man of honor, BG! And Angelina Galletta is my fuckin' daughter! And that little punk-hoodlum of yours violated my trust by sneakin' around fuckin' her! Because had he been a man, had he truly cared about her and felt that it was okay for them to be doin' what they were doin', he would've talked to me about it — like a man. I should not have had to find out about them by runnin' the prints that I lifted from his fuckin' apartment."

BG understood, Tony was one hundred percent correct, but he wasn't alone in his actions. Angelina was a grown woman and should be held accountable also. "Tony, I feel you, but Angelina's just as much at fault here. I mean —"

"BG," Tony said, cutting him off. "With all due respect, fuck off with your little speech. I really care about you and respect you as a man, but 'til you find out that your daughter's getting fucked by a man that's pretendin' to honor you, don't tell me how to feel, because you have not a fuckin' clue... And you keep that little gigolo away from me and Angelina, or I swear before Christ and all of the saints, I'll put a bullet in him... I fuckin' mean it." Tony walked over to his car and retrieved a legal envelope from the front seat. He tossed it to BG and pulled off.

BG slowly opened the envelope, already knowing what he was going to see. The first mug-shot was of Angelina, the second was of King, and the third belonged to Gemo. And the only reason Mariah's had not showed up was because she did not have a criminal record, so she had no finger prints on file. *But she does have a criminal mind*, BG mused, and he had no doubts that she had set up the whole robbery...

BOOK 4OUR

"Every man must journey through hell to reach his paradise."

—Anonymous

THE APOCALYPSE

Chapter 32

THREE O'CLOCK

Mane knew that he was wrong. But how could he just walk away from Angelina? He respected her father and realized now that he and Angelina should have handled the situation differently, but they both were afraid that Tony would not have understood. After all, they were Italian and he was black. They were law abiding, tax paying citizens and he was a lawless thug. So nobody could have ever told him that Tony would have allowed him to date his daughter.

Sadam sat on the passenger side as Mane zipped the Aston Martin through traffic.

The sky was dark, though it was only three o'clock.

Rain.

The clouds were thick.

Mane hoped to make it to the mall on 163rd Street before the bottom fell out of the sky.

Angelina.

She had promised to meet him there.

To see him again.

He did not want to disregard or disrespect Tony, but truthfully, he really loved Angelina. And it was a shame that it took for him to lose her in order for him to realize just how much he adored her. Mane cherished the time they had spent together. He missed the things she did to him, longed to do the thing that he'd once done to her.

Adrift.

He was lost in the affinity of their memories.

Remorseful.

Literally sick at the thought of what he had lost... But he had not lost her completely. Because she had agreed to meet with him. Which meant that she probably still loved him.

Mane whipped up into the parking garage at the mall and drove up to the third level. Seeing the black 370Z, he quickly parked four spaces down and jumped out. A black Mercedes-Benz CLS 550 pulled in behind him. Four big white men in suits got out. But Mane never saw them, his complete focus was on Angelina. She had already gotten out of her car and was walking towards him, Sadam at his side. They were about fifteen feet away from each other when Mane noticed the startled expression of her face.

Mane quickly peeked over his shoulder and saw the men reaching. "Sadam!" Mane yelled, running as he pulled his own gun.

Angelina stood frozen.

Sadam spun around, .40 already drawn. Without blinking an eye he began letting off. *Boom! Boom! Boom! Boom! Boom! Boom!* The barrage of bullets lifted two of the suited men, sending their dead bodies sprawling to the hard concrete.

The two remaining suites returned fire. *Boom! Boom! Boom! Boom! Boom! Boom!*

Sadam's small body ate the slugs. He fell, still firing. *Boom! Boom! Boom! Boom!*

Another suite went down, leaving Sadam and three of the attackers dead.

Boom! Boom! Boom! The last of the four men fired.

The bullets barely missed Mane as he pulled Angelina down and around her car. *Boom! Boom! Boom!* Mane fired back, before turning to Angelina. "Lina, get in the damn car! We gotta go!"

With shaking hands, she opened the car door and slid in.

Mane knew that his little partner was dead. He fired off three more shots and dove in the car as Angelina reversed the vehicle, driving wildly. The shooter had taken aim and was about to fire into the car, but had to dive out of the way or risk getting ran over. When he gathered himself to take another shot the 370Z was skirting around the corner...

Chapter 33

THREE-FIFTEEN

Gemo and King had been over to Mariah's house since six o'clock in the morning, arguing and bagging up drugs for the trap in Little Haiti. The two men had also counted out $93,000 — money from the last two shifts. It was the most money that the trap had made in one day. Gemo smiled, he was indeed happy, because he had gotten his money up and the streets were starting to feel his presence. Pressure. That's what he was bringing to the streets.

After Danielle had told him that she no longer wanted to be with him, he had really snapped, not on her, but on the streets. He had been cool with her decision, because truthfully, what he felt for Danielle, the woman that had always been there for him and had always given so unselfishly, was more so a sympathetic obligation than love. He loved the woman, how could he not — she was beautiful and loving — but he was not in love with her, not anymore. Her leaving him had only bruised his pride and blackened what was left of his heart.

Since then Gemo had bought himself a two bedroom condo on Key Biscayne, but most nights he slept in expensive hotels with different young tenders. And his days were spent at Mariah's house mixing and bagging up the product for their trap, which was making more money every day it seemed.

While the two men worked and talked about how much money they were making and how many bitches they were fucking, Mariah lay on the couch watching TV and wishing she was elsewhere. Since she'd been back from her last trip to Atlanta she had only talked to Mane once, and the conversation had been brief. She wondered what was good with him, she wanted to see him, but for some reason he was not answering his phone. For three days Mariah had been blowing up his phone and text, but he was not answering or responding. *Probably out somewhere with that loose-deep, no ass havin', skunk-ass cracka*, Mariah fumed.

Still watching TV and thinking about Mane, Mariah caught snatches of the men's conversation:

"We probably gotta send shorty back up top in like two days," Gemo said. "It's only 'bout three bricks of clean in there."

King looked surprised. "Includin' the six bricks we took from that sucka Mane?!"

Mariah really opened her ears after hearing Mane's name.

"Crazy-ass nigga, that's been over a week ago! We've spent that money two times over."

King thought about the money that the spot was pumping and how he'd been spending money and realized that Gemo was right. "Yeah, you're right, bruh... That shit's comin' and goin' fast. But, umm, you don't wanna swing back by there and see if the lil' nigga's stupid enough to still be usin' the same *lay low* that we followed him to when he dropped Mariah off that day?"

Gemo shook his head. "Nah, BG's schooled him better than that," Gemo told King, but he did not tell him that he'd already doubled back by himself and found the spot empty.

"So what's left?"

"Like three bricks of girl and a brick of boy."

King had the heroin plug. "Aiight, I'ma hit my peoples and make that happen, probably snatch 'bout six of them bitches."

Gemo nodded. "And I'll hit the people in A-Town, get shorty outta here tomorrow night, because I don't wanna run out."

"Aiight, but did you think about the other spot? 'Cause for real, kid, we can open that bitch and really be eatin'! I already got the people lined up, they're waitin' on me."

"On 66th Street and 18th?"

"Yeah."

It was a busy spot. "We'll see."

King stood up. "I'm hungry as fuck. Let's go eat."

"Man, kid, we gotta finish this shit."

"Gemo, that shit ain't goin' nowhere, but I am!" King looked over at Mariah laying on the couch, her thick legs bussed open, and decided to try his hand. "How 'bout you, Mariah, let's go get room service." He wanted to fuck the pretty red-bone so bad. He had offered her $5,000 just yesterday.

Mariah simply ignored his stupid-ass like she always did.

"Keep playin' hard to get," King capped and started for the door. "You fuck 'round and don't get got."

Gemo watched his lazy-ass partner in crime exit the house. He knew that if he let King leave by himself it would probably be three hours before he came back. *Nah, fuck that, that nigga ain't leavin' me to do all the work*, Gemo thought as he grabbed his cell phone and started out to catch King before he left.

The sky outside was dark as Gemo exited the house.

Rain.

King had just slid into his forest-green BMW 750Li, which was parked beside Gemo's gray Range Rover. Mariah's Lexus was parked in her two-car garage.

Gemo was about eight feet away from the BMW when King turned the ignition. There was a quick flash. The BMW disappeared behind a bright glow of orange and yellow. Gemo felt a wave of pressure pushing him, then a loud explosion sounded as his unconscious body slammed into the house.

* * *

Mariah lay there thinking. She could not believe what she had just heard. She could expect some bullshit like that from King's no-good-ass, but to hear that Gemo was down with such *fuckery* was beyond her; and had someone told her so and she had not heard it with her own two ears, she would not have believed it, because she truly saw Gemo as a *real stand up* type dude. To see him any different hurt her... But worse, they had followed Mane from her house, which sort of made her an accessory to the infraction and also made her culpable. Gemo and King had made her a culprit in their game. *Fuck -ass niggas! That's probably why Mane ain't been dealin' with me, 'cause of these two setup-ass niggas,* she fumed. *I hope them bitches die, especially King's disrespectful, ugly, trifling-ass!*

Just as the thought appeared in her angry mind, a bright flash of orange and yellow light beamed through her window. Then a wave of pressure vibrated her house, like a mini-earthquake had occurred. *What the fuck?* she thought as the loud explosion sounded, scaring the living shit out of her. Mariah's heart was pounding as she ran to the door. She stepped out and saw the two burning vehicles in her driveway. Gemo's body was crumbled on the concrete, beside the house. *Oh my God*, Mariah thought, looking from the carnage to the street in front of her house. She saw two white men in a brown Cadillac. They were looking at the burning vehicles. The driver looked in her direction, a satisfied smirk on his big white face. He nodded at her before driving off.

Mariah was scared to death. She looked at Gemo and just knew that he was dead. *I gotta get my ass outta here before them crackas come!* she thought, running back inside. She gathered up everything that was on the table, grabbed the three kilos of cocaine and the brick of heroin that was stashed in her guest room, and all of the money that was in the house – including her own. Satisfied that she had everything, Mariah loaded the stuff in her Lexus, opened the garage, and flew up out of there. She was scared and only knew one person that she could possibly trust – she had to find Mane.

Chapter 34

THREE-EIGHTEEN

Monique ushered Devon and LG out of the house through the kitchen, into the big garage. She was running late and could not understand why BG could not drop the boys off. Now she had to go out of her way, which was going to make her late for her dress fitting. *Men!* she thought as she looked and seen that BG's BMW had her blocked in. She was about to go back in the house but decided against it. She would just drive his car.

"Come on, you two!" she fussed and slid into the car.

After adjusting the seats and mirrors, Monique hit the garage door and zoomed out.

Mary J. Blige's *Be Without You* played as she rode along. Mary was her girl. The songs that she sung over the years had helped get Monique through some tough, lonely times. But those times were now over for her. She had found love. BG was her everything. And tomorrow they would be married – until death do them part.

Excited.

Monique was so ready to be BG's wife.

Forever!

She had vowed to herself and God that she would let nothing come between her and her marriage.

The sky was so dark. *God, it's gonna rain cats and dogs*, Monique thought, hoping that the weather did not ruin her special day tomorrow.

The boys got out at the PALS Community Center and Monique sped off, not wanting to miss her appointment for the final fitting. She had spent a lot of money, well, BG had, and her dress just had to be perfect. *After all, Monique, you're only gonna do this once*, she assured herself.

When Monique parked BG's BMW in front of the dress shop in North Miami Beach, the digital clock on its dash said that it was three-fifty. Monique cursed and hopped out.

She never saw the black van that pulled in behind her, nor did she notice the three large white men that poured out of its sliding side door.

The three men, dressed in suits, briskly approached her, catching her before she reached the shop's entrance.

"Excuse me, ma'am," one of them called out, his accent foreign.

When Monique turned to see what the man wanted, she felt something hard pressed into her stomach, then an unbearable pain surged through her. Monique's bladder released as she fell forward into the man's arms.

They quickly carried her unconscious body to the van.

After placing her securely inside, the van sped off.

The entire abduction took less than thirty seconds... and no one saw a thing.

One of the men inside of the van pulled out a cell phone and placed a call. The phone only rung once before someone answered.

"Yes?"

"It was not him."

There was silence. "Who?"

"The woman, his wife... She took his car."

"So you have her?"

"Yes."
"Very well. I will call Koka."
They both hung up.

Chapter 35

THREE-FORTY

BG got dressed. Checked himself over in the full-length mirror. Smoothed out his shirt because his attire looked a little bulky. But instead of changing the shirt for a bigger one, he simply untucked it and exited the room. He still had not forgotten the old Haitian man's warning.

Exiting the house through the garage, BG decided to go in the backyard and check the palm tree. *This shit is a waste of time. I don't know why I keep doin' it,* he thought as he bent and ran his hand through the loose black soil. He felt something. A root? Couldn't be. BG gripped it and pulled hard. *What the fuck?!* BG's mind screamed. He shook the dirt off of the black pouch and pulled its drawstring open. His knees got weak and he nearly passed out when he saw Haitian Jack's Rolex inside. It looked exactly like the one he had thrown into the ocean. But no, it couldn't be… because he had thrown it into the ocean. BG looked around, suddenly paranoid. Somebody was playing games, had to be. Someone had to have put the watch there.

BG went back into the garage. Seeing that Monique had taken his car, BG jumped in his Vette, hit the garage door and peeled out. He wanted to believe that the black magic had worked and that Haitian Jack was coming home. The Voodoo priest had said that if he kept checking the palm tree and found the sign, that the black magic had worked. *This shit is crazy*, he thought, but the proof was in his hand.

Tomorrow was his big day and he could not find Gemo anywhere. He really needed to holla at his big cousin about what him and King had done to Mane. They would have to either give the bricks back or pay for them. BG had not shown Mane the fingerprint results or told him that he knew who had broken into the *lay low*. He knew that Mane would want blood, which he had every right to feel that way, but that was something that BG did not want to see, because he truly loved both of them – Mane and Gemo. But King, BG had already decided that he was going to kill him.

BG had gone by the house, but Danielle had told him that Gemo was gone, had moved out when she told him that things were not working out. Gemo was ignoring his calls. But he would find him. And when he did, Gemo would have to answer for the bullshit.

Thinking over the matter, BG figured he might be able to catch Gemo or King over in Little Haiti.

The rain had finally started. Big drops splashed the sleek Vette as BG pushed it. Meek Mill's *Black Magic* played as he rode.

He saw neither man's vehicle as he cruised by the trap on 57th Street and 6th Avenue. Continuing through the neighborhood, he spotted Mr. Fee running into the store. BG parked and ran in. He would get Mr. Fee to call him whenever he saw King or Gemo in the hood.

When BG came into the store he found Mr. Fee laughing with the store's Arab owners. Mr. Fee smiled brightly when he saw BG.

"What's up, y'all?" BG greeted them.

The store owners spoke.

Mr. Fee walked over. "Hello, my young son… What do you have for me?"

BG laughed. "You don't change, do you, Mr. Fee?"

"Sometimes, BG, but not too often," the old Haitian man replied. "You will learn that nothing in this life happens by accident." He nodded, thought. "I had to learn this the hard way. And that was before I knew that the hard way was the only way to true knowledge and understanding."

Damn! BG thought. Mr. Fee had gone deep with that one.

Mr. Fee laughed at BG's expression. "Now, buy me a drink."

BG shook his head and started towards the coolers, which were located at the rear of the store.

No sooner than BG disappeared, a tall and very sexy white woman entered the store. Her eyes were cold blue. She wore leather pants that hugged her sexy hips and thighs. The open leather waist coat gave them a view of her sheer laced blouse, which she wore no bra underneath.

Mr. Fee stared open-mouthed.

The woman looked around the store and then walked off towards the back. The heels of her ankle boots *click-clacked* against the unfinished concrete floor as she walked. When she turned the corner that led to the coolers she spotted BG. He turned around, a bottle of cheap wine in each hand, and they locked eyes.

"Is some of that wine for me?" she asked in Hungarian.

BG frowned. He could not understand her language.

His confusion caused her to smile. She stopped right in front of him. "I like wine... But perhaps I like you more," Koka said, but this time she spoke English.

"Do I know you?" BG questioned her. This was their third encounter and he wanted to get to the bottom of things.

"No, but you know a friend of mine. His name was Andras."

BG frowned. He'd heard the name before, but couldn't quite place it.

Koka licked her lips. And quickly, before BG could react, she leaned in and kissed him hard on the lips. He tried to pull away, but

Koka had one hand on the back of his neck, holding him while she tongue-kissed him.

Dropping the two bottles of wine, BG pushed her away. "Bit—" he started to say, but froze at the sight of the little chrome, silenced .22 pistol.

Koka squeezed off all six shots, *Pzztt! Pzztt! Pzztt! Pzztt! Pzztt! Pzztt!* The sound was barely above a whisper.

BG took all six shots center mass. The impact of the burning hot lead sent BG crashing into the coolers behind him, causing the coolers' glass doors to shatter. BG bounced and fell facefirst on the floor.

Smiling seductively, Koka turned on her high heels and started for the exit.

One of the store's owners was just coming around the cash out counter as she exited the store.

Mr. Fee stole one more look at her sexy body as she walked out.

The red Lotus stopped in the pouring rain.

Koka slid in and the exotic sports car sped off.

Lifting a cell phone from the glove compartment, Koka called Kadar's phone.

"Yes?" he answered on the third ring.

"I got him."

"Good."

"What now?"

"The message has been sent. Now we wait."

"Wait?"

"Yes," Kadar told his sister and hung up before she could reply.

Chapter 36

A WEEK EARLIER

Kadar got out of the red Lotus that was being driven by his sister Koka. In his right hand was a slender briefcase. Koka got out and the two siblings entered the small downtown building.

The old Spanish secretary stood and walked around her small desk to greet him. Smiling, she shook Kadar's hand. "Hello, Mr. Kadar, how are you today?"

"I am fine," Kadar said with a straight face.

"And you, Ms. Koka? I hope that you are fine also," the woman said, shaking Koka's hand.

"I am." Koka smiled at the woman.

"Coffee, tea?"

They both declined her offer.

"Okay… Come this way. He is expecting you."

They followed the small graying woman to an office door. She knocked twice before peeking her head inside. "Your two o'clock appointment, sir."

"Good, send them in."

The woman turned, still smiling. "Go inside."

They entered and she closed the door, leaving them alone to handle whatever business it was that they had with her employer.

Koka and Kadar took seats in front of the small desk, opposite the round private investigator that sat behind it. The three of them had met on several occasions. Business. They had lots of money and a need for information, and the PI was very good at finding things out. He was an ex-FBI agent, so he knew all of the tricks and still had quite a few human resources in and around the department.

"Koka, Kadar, what can I do for you today?" he asked, eyeing them both.

"I need information on a man," Kadar answered.

"You have a name?"

"No. I have a picture."

The PI frowned. "Let's see it."

Kadar popped the briefcase and removed the still shots that he had recovered from the security system's hard drive. He tossed the pictures onto the desk.

The private investigator picked them up. Leaned back in his chair and studied the pictures, one after the other. Frowned. "There's two men here. Which one are you asking about?"

"Either one."

The PI nodded, brushed at the stubble on his chin. "What's the info worth to you, Kadar? Depending on the job, my rates get as high as $250 an hour."

Kadar reached into the briefcase and removed a bundle of money. Without speaking, he tossed the money on the desk just as he had tossed the pictures.

The PI smiled. Picked up the money, which looked to be about $5,500, and dropped it in a desk drawer next to a black .45 automatic. He then leaned forward and spread the pictures out. "This guy here," he said, pointing at the picture. "His name's Gemo. Runs around in the Little Haiti area. Just got out of the federal penitentiary. Pretty shrewd fella. Loves money. So if some's missing or you're looking to make some, you've fingered the right guy."

"How do you know so much about him?"

The PI went in another desk drawer and removed an envelope. He opened it and laid it on the desk. "Because of him." He pointed at a picture of a man that looked like he could have been Gemo's brother. "This, my friend, is BG. And he's even more intelligent and conniving than Gemo. The two are first cousins."

Kadar nodded. "You mind if I —"

The PI shook his head. "No, go right ahead, take the whole file."

Placing the envelope and the still shots into the briefcase, Kadar closed it and stood.

Koka stood with him.

"You have been a great help, Mr. Gomez," Kadar said.

Gomez wondered what was Kadar's interest in Gemo and BG, but decided not to ask. BG had cost Gomez his career as an FBI agent and Gomez hated him. He had vowed to one day kill BG. Maybe Kadar would save him the trouble.

"Just doing my job, Kadar... You need me for anything else, I'm here."

Kadar nodded.

Gomez stood and walked them to the door. He always liked to watch Koka walk in front of him. The way her hips swayed, like she was a model on the runway. And her ass? It was absolutely perfect.

"You two be careful with those guys," Gomez stated.

Koka just looked at him. Her eyes told the PI that *those guys had better be careful with her*.

Kadar almost smiled. "As a businessman, Mr. Gomez, I learned that to underestimate the risk, at any level of an endeavor, is to increase that risk... So, Mr. Gomez, I'm always careful."

Well, excuse the hell out of me, Mr. Philosopher, Gomez thought to himself, but said to Kadar, "Nice, I'll try to remember that."

"Please do," Kadar turned, unsmiling, and exited.

Koka followed, her lithe body swaying provocatively as she walked.

Gomez allowed himself exactly ten seconds of lustful contemplation before turning to his secretary and saying, "Those two have really got their hands full."

THREE HOURS LATER

The big six-foot-four, 250 pound Hungarian stood before his followers. They were all congregated at a large round table. The air was charged with nervous anticipation.

With his cold blue eyes moving from face to face, Kadar measured every man and woman that sat before him. Beside Kadar, the new leader of the Hungarian Mafia, stood his *consulere*, Ferenc. Ferenc was a small, nervous man. His eyes were dark and large. At age 47, Ferenc had seen a lot in his years as a member of the Hungarian Mafia. Leadership had come and gone, yet Ferenc was still here. The small, nervous man with the full-head of gray hair was a survivor.

Standing opposite Ferenc, on Kadar's other side, stood Koka, Kadar's sister and second in command. Koka stood an even six-foot tall and weighed a sexy 133 pounds. Since junior high school Koka had trained in martial arts and conditioned her body strenuously. So she wasn't just sexy, she was deadly. Her eyes were a cold blue just like her brother's. She also wore her silky black hair cut low, military *buzz-cut* and spiked on the top, just like her brother's. With measurement of 32-24-36, pale white skin and small lips, Koka was every man's desire.

As a rule, every man or woman in attendance wore black suits and ties. The Hungarian Mafia was one of the world's oldest mobs and their discipline was strict.

"Do you all know why I have called you here today?" Kadar asked. His Hungarian accent heavily pronounced.

Everyone nodded their heads. They all knew that Andras Simonyi, their previous leader and Kadar's mentor, had been murdered along with his beautiful wife April Simonyi. And though Andras' murder had placed Kadar at the head of their organization, it was easy to see that he was saddened by the event and wanted blood as a result.

"I know who is responsible for this." He nodded his head. An evil frown covered his pale face. Kadar was only 29-years-old, but looked as if he were 40. The corners of his *buzz-cut* were gray and he had crow's feet on the corner of his cold eyes. "I want them dead."

Again, everybody nodded their agreement.

"Now, none of you knows this, but when our beloved Andras was murdered, three million dollars in rare diamonds were stolen," Kadar informed the captains of his mob.

A loud murmur buzzed throughout the room as the wide-eyed members discussed the newfound revelation. The Hungarian mob dealt in all sorts of vice: extortion, human trafficking, prostitution, and murder for hire. But *blood diamonds* were their main source of income. And three million dollars' worth was a substantial amount.

After allowing them a few minutes to vent, Kadar began speaking again. "I've heard from my sources that a large amount of drugs was somehow surrounding this whole mess. I also have the surveillance tapes from Andras' house cameras. The people are Americans. Niggers! And I want them dead!" Kadar said, adding a string of obscenities in his native Hungarian language. "And I want those diamonds back!"

Kadar was furious. He removed his black suit coat and tugged at his black tie. The thin silk shirt stretched and strained to contain Kadar's twenty-inch biceps and huge pectoral muscles. A big gray-steel .50 caliber Desert Eagle was holstered beneath his left armpit.

A senior member of the board cleared his throat. The old Hungarian was bald and chubby. Liver spots marked his round face. "Kadar, it's forbidden for *any* member of this board to deal in drugs, and that especially goes for the *don*. Rules were put in place to safeguard this organization and to distinguish us from common nigger and spic gangs! So if Andras broke those rules and laid with *nigger-dogs*, who are we to involve ourselves because he got bit? I don't think this —"

Kadar pulled the big gun from its holster, causing the man to fall silent. His eyes bulged as Kadar briskly approached him. The room was dead quiet. Kadar grabbed the man about the throat and forced the long barrel into the man's mouth. Once the barrel was firmly in place, Kadar pulled the trigger. *Doom!* the big gun roared, sending the man's brains and the entire back of his skull splattering the tiled floor.

A nervous murmur echoed through the room.

Kadar had set his mark. He was the new leader – the only leader. And he was not to be questioned on any level.

Before moving back to the head of the room, Kadar signaled for some of his men to clean up the mess that the dead man had caused.

"Now," he said, "Does anyone else wish to disrespect Andras Simonyi, my mentor, in his absence?"

Nobody uttered a word.

That pleased Kadar, because he did not wish to kill another member of the congregation.

Kadar signaled and the lights went out. A picture of both BG and Gemo appeared on the wall.

"This man," he said, pointing at BG, "is BG. And the other man is his cousin, Gemo. These two are the men who robbed and killed Andras Simonyi and his wife... They lead a highly efficient gang called the ROC and they operate out of a club called Wet Wetz."

Everybody nodded. They were paying close attention.

"Koka, my sister and second in command, will lead the reconnaissance and formulate the plan of attack... I want them dead! But most of all, I want those diamonds back... No excuses! I don't care what you have to do, who you have to kill or payoff, just get me those diamonds. Understood?"

The members of the Hungarian Mafia nodded their agreement.

Kadar and Koka left the room...

Gift And The Curse

I'm damned if I do and damned if I don't,
Either way this life is a double-edged sword.

Nothing can prepare you for the drama and stress that money brings, when there's so much that you can't afford.

Yeah, we thought it would get easier the more cash we had, but being naïve back then we just did not know,

That this lifestyle we're living is a Gift and a Curse, and I find myself wishing at times that I was broke.

Looking forward, I'm always looking back, to see how I got to this point in my life.

Wish I had a receipt to take this bullshit back, because some things carry too high a price.

With no choice in the matter, I take the bad with the good, but no matter the weight, I'm here standing at the scratchline.

So if you were with me before, then ride with me now,

And *Get It How We Live* one more time...

Poem by Roderrick Vann

Story continued in Get It How You Live Vol. 4

Money Power Respect

PLEX PRESENTS:
NO TURNING...

Nathan "Big Nation" Welch

PLEX PRESENTS
LOVE & THUGGIN

BY BO BROWN

CRUMBS TO BRICKS

BY CAPO CAT

GOLDIE

CASHMAN
DUVAL CO

Part One

sOmEThInG 2 DiE 4

A Classic Novel
By PLEX

A Novel By

PLEX PRESENTS

YOUNG -N- THUGGIN

The Troy Jones Story. Written by PLEX & Troy Disco Jones

BADLAND PUBLICATIONS
PO Box 11623
Riviera Beach, FL 33419-1623

Shipping address
Name:

_____

Address:

_____

City: _____ State: _____ Zip: _____

Title	Author	Price
STREET RAISED: The Begin...	Mike Harper	15.95
BOO BABY: The Secret Of...	PLEX	15.95
STREET RAISED: The Raw Deal	PLEX	15.95
BUCKIN' DA' DICE Vol. 1	BOOK GANG	15.95
NO TURNING...	Big Nation	13.95
ONE LOVE	PLEX	13.95
SUGAR	Mike Harper	15.95
LOVE & THUGGIN	Bo Brown	15.95
CRUMBS TO BRICKS	Capo Cat	15.95
EROTIC DESIRES	BOOK GANG	13.95
PROMISCUOUS	PLEX & C. Williams	10.95
GET IT HOW YOU LIVE	Big Gemo	13.95
GET IT HOW YOU LIVE VOL2	Big Gemo & PLEX	13.95
sOmEtHiNg 2 DiE 4	PLEX	14.95
Young-N-Thuggin	Troy Jones & PLEX	14.95
LIL ONE: Blood Investment	K–1 & Bino	15.00

3.75 (S&H) for 1-5 Books _____

For quantities over 5 add $ .75 per book _____